THE MERMAIDS OF ELDORIS

BOOKS 1-6

PJ RYAN

PJRYANBOOKS.COM

BOOK 1: MICHELLE

ONE

Under the sea, things rarely moved fast. Fish glided through the water. The currents flowed peacefully. Mermaids swam in and out of the rock formations that sprouted up from the sand in the deepest water.

To Michelle, it was wonderful—until it was time for a crowning. Then everything moved so fast that Michelle could barely keep up with it. Normally she was excited for the adventure and festivities, but this time was different.

Michelle smoothed down the scarf that her sister had just draped around her shoulders. It was as blue as the water all around her.

"I'm sorry, I couldn't find the pink one." Arianna swam around behind her and fixed a twist in the scarf. "I think this one is perfect, though."

"It's fine." Michelle's heart pounded. She wished she wasn't wearing any scarf at all.

"Aren't you excited?" Arianna twisted her finger through her sister's hair. "You're going to get your crown!"

"Sure." Michelle smiled as she looked up at her sister. "It'll be great."

"She doesn't sound excited." Her other sister, Harriet, put her hands on her hips. "Michelle, have you practiced your song?"

"Yes, yes, I have." Michelle crossed her fingers. She hadn't gotten past the first part of the melody she was meant to sing at the crowning.

"Good job." Arianna smiled.

"She's lying." Harriet crossed her arms. "Michelle, you can't mess this up. Father and Mother will be so upset if you do."

"She'll do fine. Leave her alone!" Arianna waved her hand through the water and sent a ripple of bubbles straight at Harriet's face.

"Fine, let her lie to you. The truth will come out soon enough." Harriet flicked her tail through the water and sent a ripple of water back at Arianna as she left.

"Don't let her get to you. I'm sure you'll do just fine." Arianna smiled as she looked at her little sister. "Tomorrow is a special day for you. Smile."

"I don't want to smile." Michelle flicked her tail and pulled away from her sister. "I don't think I want to do this."

"Michelle, you don't have a choice." Arianna stared at her. "You're a princess and you must be crowned."

"And then what?" She shook her head. "I won't be able to swim off on my own anymore. I won't be able to play games with Trina and Kira. I'll just have to stay inside the palace grounds."

"It's for your safety." Arianna frowned. "Being a princess comes with many important jobs, but it also puts you at risk. You know that Father has enemies in the sea that would like to see someone else be king. They'd stop at nothing to make that happen."

"But I'm not afraid." Michelle sighed. "I'm more afraid of being stuck in one place than I'll ever be of Father's enemies. I mean, have you ever actually seen any of them?" She crossed her arms as she stared at her sister. "I know we've all heard the stories since we were babies, but have you ever seen one of these scary creatures that Father claims are out there?"

"No, I haven't."

"Because they're not real!"

"Because Father keeps us safe!" Arianna frowned. "You're too young to know better. There are horrible creatures out there and the very worst are a kind you never want to meet—a kind that will put you in a cage and never set you free. Humans."

"They are a myth!" Michelle laughed. "Even Ellen says so."

"Ellen thinks she knows a lot about everything, but she's never been off the palace grounds." Arianna flicked her tail sharply in the water, sharp enough to create a shower of tiny bubbles. "Humans are real. I know they are and Father does too. You'd better not let him hear you talking like this."

"It's silly to think so." Michelle gazed off through the endless water all around her. "To think that there is an entire world above the water. A place where people walk instead of swim and breathe through their noses instead of gills. It doesn't make much sense, does it, Arianna?"

"If Father says it's true, then I know it's true." Arianna looked into her sister's eyes. "You will be at your crowning tomorrow, Michelle, and you'll do as Father says."

"Don't I have any choice? What if I don't want to be a princess? What if I don't want to be safe?" She turned away from her sister.

"Well, we all love you too much not to keep you safe." Arianna gave her a warm hug. "You're just nervous. You'll do fine. Don't let Harriet worry you. I'll be back to check on you later." Arianna swam off through the water in the direction of the main palace.

The palace grounds stretched as far as Michelle could see.

The rocks towered up through the water, covered in coral and sea life. It was a beautiful home.

But when Michelle looked at it, all she saw was a prison. Once she was crowned, she would be expected to follow the rules of every princess. And Michelle had never been good at following rules.

As she swam away from the palace, she wondered what it would be like to explore—to really explore. To swim further than she'd ever swam before.

She often listened to the stories of older mermaids. They would tell tales of other places in the sea, places where the water was warmer or colder, places where the sand was a different color and the sea plants glowed.

All of it sparked her curiosity. All of it made her want to see it for herself.

But that was not her destiny.

Her destiny was to be one of the three princesses of Eldoris, a vast expanse that her father ruled over.

It was a beautiful and peaceful place. But could it ever be enough for her?

TWO

Michelle plucked at the sand, then dug her fingers into it. Usually playing with the sand helped her to relax. Today, it didn't help much. Each moment that passed brought her closer to the big day.

"There you are!" Trina swooped down through the water and landed with a puff of sand right beside her. "I've been looking for you everywhere!"

"I told you she'd be here." Kira plopped down on the other side of Michelle. "She always hides out near the caves when she's upset."

"I do?" Michelle's eyes widened.

"You do." Kira crossed her arms over her knees and looked at Michelle. "It's the crowning, isn't it?"

"It is." Michelle frowned and dug her fingers into the sand again.

"Why don't we go hunt some jellyfish?" Trina nudged her with her elbow. "That always makes you feel better."

"That does sound like fun." Michelle smiled at her friend. "But I don't have my net with me."

"I do." Trina snapped her fingers and a net appeared in her hand. "You can use mine."

"There's no time to catch jellyfish! Michelle needs to get ready for her crowning." Kira crossed her arms.

"No way!" Trina grinned. "She needs to have nonstop fun! After the crowning, she'll have all those rules to follow. But until tomorrow, she's still free!"

"Exactly." Michelle looked up at her friends. "I do want to have fun. It might be the last fun I ever have."

"Don't think that way." Kira hugged her. "Being a princess is very special. Trina and I will never be princesses. And you'll always be safe inside the palace. The guards will protect you. You'll get to learn so much."

"I know all those things." Michelle frowned. "But what if I don't want to be safe? What if I want to see everything that's out there?" She looked off through the expanse of water. "There's so much more, don't you think? So much that we've never seen before?"

"I don't know. I kind of like it here." Kira whispered. "I know some of the things that are out there. Sharks." She shivered. "Giant squids." She closed her eyes tight. "And worst of all —lobsters!"

"Lobsters are worst of all?" Trina giggled. "What's so bad about lobsters? I would love to have one as a pet!"

"Ah! You're nuts!" Kira covered her face. "Their googly eyes and their clacking claws? How terrible!"

"Clacking claws?" Trina snapped her teeth together. "Like that? Does it sound like that?" She snapped her teeth again.

"Trina!" Kira gasped and covered her ears.

"Alright, alright!" Michelle laughed. "I know there are probably some scary things out there. But for every scary thing, I'll bet there are wonderful things too." She sighed and looked back out through the water. "Is it so wrong that I want to find out?"

"It's not wrong." Trina frowned, then hugged Michelle. "But it might not be possible."

"It's just not fair." Michelle swam up out of the sand. She swirled her tail through the water with a sharp snap. "Maybe I just don't want to be a princess!"

"Only you wouldn't want to be a princess." Kira looked back toward the coral palace. "I'd love to live inside the palace. It's sure better than mining for sea stones. That's the future I have."

"But it doesn't have to be. You could explore if you wanted to." Michelle swooped down to her. "You could go anywhere, see everything!"

"Be eaten by a shark! Remember?" Kira rolled her eyes. "No thanks. I'd take a nice fluffy bed in the palace any day."

"I wish we could switch places." Michelle crossed her arms. "Then we would both be happy."

"But we can't." Kira looked into her eyes. "Michelle, you're my best friend. I want you to be happy, but, if you keep dreaming like this, you never will be. The truth is, you are a princess and you are going to be crowned and then you will live in the palace. It's time you just got used to it. Just like the rest of us have to get used to the futures we have. It's just the way it is. It's the way it has to be."

"Why?" Michelle punched the water in front of her. "Why does it have to be that way?"

"It's how it's always been." Trina shrugged. "I don't know why."

"Look!" She pointed at the coral that grew on a piece of rock that jutted out of the sand. "Do you see that coral?"

"Yes." Trina looked at the coral. "What about it?"

"When I first came here, it was just a tiny dot. But over time it's gotten bigger and bigger. Just like me. Just like you and Kira. The ocean doesn't stay the same and neither do we, so why do the rules have to always stay the same?" She snapped her tail. "I'm going to find out!"

As she swam through the water she barely heard Kira call out to her.

"Michelle, don't upset your mother!"

Michelle ignored the warning and swam as swiftly as she could back toward the palace. She often raced her friends and most of the time she won. She loved to swim fast. But in the palace, there was nowhere to swim fast without running into rock.

In the palace she would be stuck in the same places forever.

THREE

Michelle burst through the seaweed that covered the entrance to the throne room. It was the same place she would receive her crown the next day. The walls sparkled with sea stones of all different colors.

Two large shells sat in the center of the room, each lined with soft sand. Her mother perched on one, her tail curled up alongside of her. Her head rested on her hand as she gazed up through the open hole in the top of the throne room.

Schools of fish swam by, their silver scales flickering in the beams of light that filtered down through the water.

"Mother!" Michelle swam up to her. "I have to talk to you!"

"Not now, Michelle." Her mother waved her hand. "I'm resting. I need to be ready for the crowning tomorrow."

"But Mother, that's what I need to talk to you about." Michelle swam closer. Her mother's long hair flowed through the water. In Michelle's mind, she looked like a pearl—perfect and impossible to get to.

"What is it?" Her mother finally looked at her. "Oh, Michelle, what have you done to your hair? Your sisters will have to fix it before tomorrow."

"Please, Mother, I need to know—will I have to stay in the palace forever after I'm crowned?"

"You already know that, dear." Her mother sat up and looked at her. "It's so sweet that you're nervous. Come up here with me." She patted the soft sand in her shell.

"Mother, I'm not nervous." Michelle curled up beside her. "Is it really forever? Don't you ever leave the palace?"

"It is forever." Her mother trailed her fingers through her hair. "It's the only way to make sure that we are all safe."

"But why is it a rule?" Michelle frowned. "Who decided it the first time?"

"Your grandfather."

"My grandfather?" Michelle stared at her mother. "But I don't have a grandfather."

"You did." Her mother draped her arm around her shoulder. "He knew how dangerous the ocean was. He knew better than anyone. He made the rule to keep the royal family safe, because that's the only way we can keep the rest of the mermaids safe. There is so much danger out there."

"Sharks? Mother, most sharks don't want to hurt us. If we leave them alone, they leave us alone. The really scary creatures live in the deep dark sea, not here, where the light shines through." She looked up through the hole in the ceiling. "Is there really so much to be afraid of?"

"Yes, my darling." Her mother kissed the top of her head. "So much that we know about and even more that we don't. But don't worry. After tomorrow, you'll never have to be afraid. You will be safe in the palace with the rest of us and one day you will have a daughter whom you will keep safe as well."

"No!" Michelle pulled away from her mother. "I won't! I won't ever make her stay in one place."

"Michelle." Her mother swam toward her. "You will get used to it. You'll see how wise it is."

"No, I won't!" She swam away from her. "I don't want to be a princess, Mother! I don't want to be stuck in this palace forever! I don't care what Grandfather said!"

"Do not speak that way about him!" her mother shouted, which made the water all around her ripple. The waves carried swiftly in all directions and slammed into the palace walls, which made the entire palace tremble. "Your grandfather was a wonderful, wise man!"

"Then what happened to him?" Michelle shivered as she watched her mother swim toward her. It wasn't often that she saw her mother get angry, but when she did, it scared her. It scared everyone who saw it. "If the palace keeps us all safe, then what happened to Grandfather?"

"He broke his rule. He went out into the ocean—into the beyond—and he never came back!" The walls shook again.

Her mother closed her eyes. She swayed back and forth in the water. When she spoke again, her voice was softer.

"I'm sorry, Michelle, but you are a princess. You are part of this family. Being part of this family means that it is your job to protect all the mermaids, and the only way that you can do that is to keep yourself safe. It may seem unfair now, but one day you will understand." She touched her daughter's cheek. "I love you, but these are the rules, and they're not going to change. Tomorrow you will be crowned and you will become a protector of all the mermaids—of all your friends and of all the beings that live in our world. Don't you think that's something to be proud of?"

"I'm sure it is." Michelle looked down at the rock floor beneath her. "But it's not what I want." She looked back up at her mother. "I just want to explore."

"Never." Her mother stared hard into her eyes. "Do you hear me, Michelle? You will never explore. It's time you put those silly ideas out of your head. It's time you grew up."

"Mother, please—"

"No!" The walls shook again, this time so hard that a few of the sea stones tumbled out of the rock.

"You will stay in your shell until it's time for the crowning." Her mother pointed to the seaweed door. "Go! Now!"

Her voice was so powerful that the force of it carrying through the water pushed Michelle back through the door. She grabbed the rock wall just as she would have passed through it.

"Mother?" Her voice softened.

"Go, Michelle!" Her mother turned away from her.

"I'm sorry about Grandfather," she whispered. "You must have been so sad when you lost him."

"Yes, Michelle. Yes, I was." She swam back toward her shell and curled up again. She looked back at the open spot in the ceiling.

Michelle watched as the light that filtered through the water flickered against her mother's skin. She looked like a jewel, like the sea stones in the wall.

Maybe her mother was right about everything.

FOUR

That night as Michelle tried to sleep, she kept seeing the flickering on her mother's skin. It was just a trick of light and the fish swimming by, but to her it seemed like so much more.

Her mother spent all her time cooped up in the palace. She claimed to be happy, but she never looked happy to Michelle. In fact, most of the time, Michelle thought she looked pretty sad.

Would that be her one day as her mother said? Would she have the same talk with her own daughter? She shivered at the thought. Yes, that was a long time in the future, but that future would be set in stone the next day.

As her thoughts continued to swirl, she swam out of bed. She looked out through a small window in the stone wall of her room and saw a distant glow.

What was it? A shiny creature? A pocket of moonlight that managed to make its way through the water?

She had no idea, and if she was crowned, she never would.

Her heart pounded as she made a decision. She gathered a few things around her room, snapped her fingers, and watched the objects disappear. They would travel with her and be at her fingertips when she needed them.

She looked back out the window. The glow had faded, but her choice stayed the same.

When everyone gathered for the crowning the next day, there would be one mermaid missing. She just had to get past her mother.

As she crept out of her room, she peered down the corridor in search of anyone who might catch her. For a moment, she thought about going right back to her shell.

There were a million things to be afraid of, things she knew about and things she could never imagine. Yes, it was scary. But it could also be amazing. She had to know what was out there, even if it meant leaving the only world she knew behind.

After one last moment of hesitation, she swam forward and right out into the open water. It wouldn't be long before she was missed. She had to get as far as she could, otherwise the guards would find her.

As she reached the edge of the palace grounds, she looked back over her shoulder. She thought about her parents and her sisters. Her heart ached when she thought of leaving Trina and Kira behind. They had all been best friends since they were tiny mermaids. She would miss them the most.

Still, she swam forward. She had never heard of anyone leaving the safety of the mermaid world. But she knew that one merman had. Her grandfather. But he hadn't come back either.

Was that because he'd gotten lost? Encountered a terrible danger? Or did he come across something too wonderful to swim away from?

The further she swam, the more certain she became that she would not turn back. Adventure awaited her!

She charged through the water in the direction of the glow that she'd seen. Maybe it was nothing more than some glowing coral, but maybe—maybe it was to be her first adventure.

She swam until she couldn't see the palace anymore. As the

water grew deeper and darker, her heart pounded faster. She'd never been so far away from home before.

Exhausted from swimming so fast, she stretched out on a large flat rock. She knew she had to keep moving, but a little rest couldn't hurt. She closed her eyes and felt the water flow over her skin.

When she opened her eyes again, she saw a squid making its way toward her. Her eyes widened. Squids were not allowed past the boundaries of the mermaid world. The guards made sure of it. She had always been told they were quite dangerous.

It was too late to hide. It swam closer and closer.

She remained very still. Maybe the squid would think she was part of the rock.

"Why, hello there." The squid's long tentacles drifted through the water in her direction.

He wasn't the biggest squid she'd ever seen, but he certainly wasn't the smallest. He was bigger than she was. With her focus on the creature in front of her, she almost forgot about the darkness all around her and the many other creatures that could sneak up behind her.

"H-hello."

"Are you lost?" The squid swam a little closer.

"No." She shivered. "Well, I don't actually know where I am, but I'm not lost."

"That seems impossible." The squid smiled. "I'll take you back to the Coral Palace."

"No." She drew back. "I don't want to go back."

"What do you mean?" He swung his tentacles through the water. "It's not safe for you to be out here. I'll take you back right now."

"No!" She backed up again until she bumped into the rock she had been lying on. "I'm not going back."

"You've run away?" He sank down to the sand. "How brave!

How foolish!" He crept closer to her along the sand. "All alone in the deep? Why, there are so many dangers."

"Stay back!" Michelle swam up into the water away from him.

"Frightened, are you?" He swung his long tentacles through the water, which stirred it up.

"Please stop that!" Michelle twirled in the fast current he'd created. As she spun around, she realized she might have made a terrible mistake.

FIVE

"Now!" someone shouted as Michelle continued to spin.

Through the bubbles and sloshing water, she made out two mermaids as they tangled thick sea grass around the squid's arms.

Michelle finally stopped spinning. Still dizzy, she swam toward the two mermaids.

"Let me go!" The squid tried to get free of the grass.

"No way!" Trina crossed her arms. "You shouldn't have been messing with our friend!"

"Michelle, are you okay?" Kira swam over to her.

"I think so." Michelle stared at them both. "How did you find me?"

"We followed you." Trina smiled. "We saw you sneak out."

"You did? But I was so careful." Michelle frowned.

"We were going to surprise you and take you out for a swim with the jellyfish before your crowning. But we saw you sneak out, so we thought we should follow you." Kira looked into her eyes. "Is what he said true? Were you really going to run away?"

"Not going to. I did." Michelle swam closer to her friends. "I don't want to be a princess. I just want to be free."

"A princess?" The squid wiggled in the grass. "Dear me, dear me, you shouldn't be out here all alone! I was only going to take you back! Now I *must* take you back—right this second!" He broke free of the grass. "Let's go—and hurry!"

"No, no, no!" Michelle ducked under his swinging arms. "I won't go back, not ever!"

"Not ever?" Kira stared at her. "What about your sisters and your parents?"

"What about us?" Trina grabbed Michelle's hand.

"I will miss you all so much, but once that crown is placed on my head, I won't ever be free again. I have to do what my heart tells me to. I have to explore!" She flipped her tail through the water. "I can't expect you to understand, but you can't stop me!"

"We don't want to stop you." Trina swam around her. "But if you're going to go, we're going with you! Right, Kira?"

"Run away?" Kira shook her head. "I'm not sure that's such a good idea."

"It isn't." The squid swam in a slow circle around the three of them. "The open sea is a dangerous place. It's nowhere for three mermaids to wander."

"As long as we stick together, we'll be fine." Trina wrapped her arm around Michelle's shoulder. "What do you say, Kira? Are you going back or are you coming on an adventure with us?"

"You two should go home." Michelle frowned. "I don't want you to get in trouble because of me."

"No way." Kira crossed her arms. "Trina is right. If you're going, we're going."

"This is a terrible idea." The squid sank down into the sand. "I warned you. Remember that."

"Don't worry about him." Trina tipped her head toward the open water. "Let's go see what we can find."

"Are you sure?" Michelle glanced between her friends. "If we get caught, we'll all be in a lot of trouble."

"We're sure." Kira linked her arm through Michelle's. "You lead the way, adventurer!"

"Okay!" Michelle grinned.

As she began to swim off, she looked back once over her shoulder. The squid watched her from his perch in the sand. He didn't try to stop them or hurt them. Maybe he had been telling the truth, that he didn't want to cause them harm, that he just wanted to protect them. But she didn't want to be protected.

She swam swiftly through the water, with her friends just behind her. Now that she wasn't alone, she was even more excited to see what the open sea might have in store for her.

"Catch!" Trina called out as she tossed a round shell through the water.

"Got it!" Kira caught the shell, then tossed it into the water toward Michelle.

Michelle gave it a hard whack with her tail and the shell sailed through the water ahead of them.

"I'm getting it!" Kira laughed as she blasted past Michelle and hit the shell back toward her just before it could fall into the sand.

"Got it!" Michelle laughed and lunged for it.

"No, you don't!" Trina swooped in front of her and knocked the shell back toward Kira.

Kira swam backwards as she tried to catch it. "Got it, got it, got it!" she shrieked.

"Kira!" Michelle's eyes widened as she watched a dark cloud form in the water just behind Kira.

"Kira! Come back!" Trina shouted.

"Got it!" Kira laughed as she caught the shell in her hands. Then she looked at her friends. "What? What is it?"

"Don't move!" Michelle swam slowly toward her.

"Why not?" Kira looked over her shoulder and saw nothing but inky darkness. "Oh no!" She closed her mouth tight.

Maybe the squid they had met not long before was friendly, but this creature that had spewed its ink out into the water was not.

"Kira! Swim away from it!" Michelle called out to her.

"I'm trying!" Kira tried to swim forward, but she couldn't. Something had wrapped around her, though she couldn't see what it was. "It's like I'm tangled in something!"

"We have to save her!" Michelle swam forward but stopped as the ink drifted toward her.

"We can't reach her." Trina frowned. "There has to be another way to get her out of there!"

"We'll just have to go in and get her." Michelle swam forward again, determined to get through the ink before it could poison her.

"No, Michelle!" Trina grabbed her arm and pulled her back. "You can't, you'll never make it out."

"Oh no, here comes the octopus!" Michelle's eyes widened as she saw a giant figure begin to form in the cloud of ink.

SIX

"Coming through! Excuse me, please!" A large lobster scuttled across the sand in Kira's direction.

"Wait! Don't go over there!" Michelle pointed to the cloud of ink.

"No worries! That can't hurt me!" He charged toward Kira with his claws high in the air.

"Oh no, no, no!" Kira wriggled but she didn't swim forward.

"Be still!" the lobster barked. Then he began clacking his claws at Kira.

"Don't! Yikes! He's going to cut me to bits!" Kira cried out.

"Don't hurt her!" Michelle swam toward the lobster.

"Stop snapping at her!" Trina swam after Michelle.

"Be free!" The lobster chuckled and waved his claws through the air.

"What?" Kira wriggled again, but this time she swam forward. "I'm free!" She swam as fast as she could.

Michelle and Trina each hooked an arm through Kira's and they swam as fast as they could with her.

Although Michelle didn't dare to look back, she could feel the giant presence of the octopus just behind her. She'd known this would be a risk when she set off on her adventure, but now that it was real, she was very scared.

"Those rocks!" She pointed to a pile of large rocks ahead of them. "We should be able to fit in those cracks and the octopus won't be able to reach us there."

"Yes, let's do it!" Trina swam through the slender opening first.

Kira followed after her.

Michelle was the last to try to get through. When she tried to squeeze past, she got her arm pinned up against her side. As she tried to wriggle free, she found it was impossible.

"I'm stuck!" She reached her free hand out to Kira and Trina.

"We'll get you out!" Kira tugged as hard as she could.

"It's okay, Michelle, we've got you!" Trina tugged too.

"It's not working." Michelle frowned. "I'm really stuck." She tried not to panic as she imagined the octopus swimming up behind her.

"Can you back out?" Kira gave her a firm shove.

Michelle moved a tiny bit, but not enough to get free.

"I'm not getting anywhere!" Michelle's heart pounded. She felt something slippery glide along her tail. "Oh no!" She shivered. "I think the octopus has me!"

"No, he's not getting you!" Kira wrapped her arm around Michelle's.

Trina did the same. "Michelle, we're going to get you out!"

Michelle's teeth chattered with fear as the slimy touch crawled up along her back. She did her best not to scream as it crawled down along her pinned arm.

"Maybe he can't get me out either! Maybe when he sees I'm stuck, he'll lose interest!" She hoped that was the case but as she felt the slimy touch run up and down along her arm, she doubted that he would give up.

"Michelle!" Kira shrieked. "There's something on your arm and it's not an octopus!"

"What?" Michelle twisted her head, but no matter how hard she tried, she couldn't see what was on her arm.

"It's a sea slug!" Trina giggled. "Aw, and it's so cute!"

"A what?" Michelle wriggled in fear. When she did, her arm came free and she was able to swim forward between the rocks. She swam so fast that she crashed right into Trina.

"She must have left a slime trail on your arm." Trina helped steady Michelle as she peered at the sea slug still stuck to Michelle's arm.

"It's not polite to call it slime." The sea slug rippled her long body, then crawled off of Michelle's arm and onto the back of Trina's hand. "Carlos said you might need some help."

"The coast is clear!" Carlos, the lobster, scuttled between the rocks. "That pesky octopus found better things to do!"

"Ah! Get it away from me!" Kira shrieked as she swam away from the lobster.

"Kira!" Michelle crossed her arms. "Carlos saved your life!"

"Oh, right—well—" She cleared her throat and swam a little closer. "He's still a lobster! Look at those claws!"

"Without these claws, I would never have been able to set you free." Carlos waved them through the water. "Thank you for all your help, Bea!"

"Always happy to help a mermaid." The sea slug crawled up along Trina's arm. "You three are far from home. Are you lost?"

Michelle noticed a flicker of something stuck to Carlos's claw. "What's this?" She swam over to him.

"We're exploring." Trina peered at the sea slug. "You are such a beautiful creature!"

"Thank you." Bea bowed to Trina. "So are you!"

"Carlos, what's stuck to your claw?" Michelle picked at the nearly invisible thread that floated off the end of Carlos's claw.

"Ah, this." He glared at it. "They call it fishing line."

"They?" She tugged at the fishing line until she managed to pull it free. "It's so strong, but so thin and I can barely see it!"

"That's what makes it so dangerous." Carlos frowned as the other mermaids gathered close to him. "I've found it wrapped around even the greatest of creatures. They use so much of it that it's everywhere in the sea."

"They?" Michelle frowned. "You keep saying they. What kind of magnificent creature could invent something like this?"

"They are the humans." Carlos stared at each of them in turn. "And there is nothing magnificent about them."

"Humans?" Michelle narrowed her eyes. "What are those? Some kind of shark?" She had heard her sisters mention the creatures, but she never really believed them at all.

"Actually, they look more like you." He tugged lightly at Michelle's hair with his claw. "They have hair like yours, two eyes, a nose, and a mouth—not too different from yours." He pointed to her long tail. "But instead of a tail, they have two legs."

"Legs?" Kira squeaked.

"Legs." He nodded.

"It must be hard for them to swim with those." Michelle frowned as she looked at the fishing line.

"Maybe, but it is very easy for them to walk on them." He clacked his claws. "They are land creatures."

"What?" Trina took the fishing line from Michelle to have a look. "What's a land creature?"

"They live outside the water." Carlos looked at them. "Hasn't anyone told you about the other world?"

SEVEN

"He's teasing us!" Kira rolled her eyes. "He's making up these stories to try to scare us!"

"I'm doing no such thing!" Carlos waved his claws through the water. "I can't believe that you've never been told!"

"Carlos, you shouldn't have told them either." Bea crawled off of Trina's arm and onto one of the large rocks. "The mermaids have new laws now. They are not to speak of such things."

"Not to speak of it?" Carlos shook his head. "But that's ridiculous! Mermaids must know about the dangers of the other world! They must know in order to be safe!"

"Tell me." Michelle swam toward him. "I want to know everything!"

"Don't believe him, Michelle!" Kira crossed her arms. "If there was another world, your mother and father would have told us. Our king and queen would never lie to us!"

"King and queen." Carlos floated back away from Michelle. "You're a princess?"

"I haven't been crowned yet." Michelle waved her hand. "Never mind that, tell me about this other world!"

"I've already said too much." He looked over at Bea. "I didn't know!"

"Just zip your lips now!" Bea huffed. "You've caused enough trouble! We need to get these three home right away, before the guards come looking for them!"

"No, we're not going back." Michelle swam away from the two creatures.

"Michelle, maybe we should," Kira whispered. "Maybe it's best."

"Even if we wanted to go back, I have no idea where home is." Trina swam over to Michelle. "We've come this far and we really can't turn back."

"They can take us!" Kira pointed to the lobster and the sea slug. "Can't you?"

"Not if you don't know the way." Carlos hung his head. "I don't know exactly where the mermaid world is."

"Neither do I." Bea slid across the rock. "You three are truly lost now."

"I'm sorry that I got the two of you into this." Michelle floated down to the sand. "I wouldn't ever want either one of you to be in danger. Now we're lost and there's no way for us to get back home."

"It's not your fault." Trina settled in the sand next to her. "We knew what we were getting into when we followed you. Didn't we, Kira?"

"Uh, mostly." She edged around the lobster, then settled on the other side of Michelle. "This is adventure, isn't it? It doesn't always go the way you expect it to."

"I don't know what I thought I would find out here." Michelle looked out at the water. "Something magical, I guess. Something wonderful, maybe."

"You found me!" Carlos clacked his claws. "It doesn't get much better than that, does it?" He scuttled along the sand.

"True." Michelle laughed. "You are quite a hero, Carlos."

"I learned it from the best." He pointed a claw at Michelle. "A great adventurer, not unlike yourself. In fact, he's a mermaid too."

"A mermaid?" She stared at the lobster. "What do you mean? You've met another mermaid on an adventure?"

"Eh, is it merman?" He tipped his head from side to side. "I wasn't sure."

"Yes, actually, that's right." Michelle met his eyes. "That man you met—I think he might have been my grandfather." She swooped through the water closer to Carlos. "That must be who you mean. Do you know where he is?"

"No, I'm sorry. I haven't seen him in a very long time. One day we were on an adventure together and we were separated by a giant whale. By the time I got to the other side, he was gone. I've never seen him again."

"I can't believe this." Michelle frowned. "Not long ago I didn't even know my grandfather went missing or that another world exists. Why would my parents lie to me about all of that?"

"I'm sure they were just trying to protect you." Bea crawled along the rock toward her. "This other world—it's nothing wonderful or magical. Its full of scary, terrible creatures."

"Are you sure?" Michelle turned to look at her. "Have you seen it?"

"Well, no, but I've heard Carlos's stories and stories from others that have seen it." She shivered. "It sounds scary enough to me. I'd prefer to stay far away from it. Don't despair, princess, Carlos and I will help you find your way back home."

"I'm not a princess." Michelle narrowed her eyes. "Not yet. And I'm not going back home. I'm going to find my grandfather. I'm sure that he will tell me the truth." Michelle swam up through the water toward the crack in the rocks. "He was brave enough to explore, maybe he will be brave enough to convince my mother and father to change some of their rules."

"What if we can't find him, Michelle?" Kira swam up beside her. "Will you come back home with us then?"

"Yes." Michelle frowned. "If I can't find him, I will go back home. I promise." She looked at her two friends. "You don't have to come with me, not if you don't want to. This is my adventure and I've already put you both in danger."

"We're going." Trina smiled as she hugged her friend.

"Absolutely." Kira nodded.

"Us too!" Bea crawled onto Trina's shoulder. "Do you mind if I hitch a ride?"

"Not at all." Trina smiled at her.

"I'll do my best to keep up!" Carlos called out from the sand.

"Here." Kira swam down to him. "You can hold onto my hair."

"I can?" He stared at her. "Are you sure?"

"Yes. I'm sure." She smiled as she looped her hair around his claws. "You saved my life, the least I can do is give you a ride."

"Thank you." He smiled at her, then settled onto her back.

As Michelle led the way out of the rocks, she was glad to have two new friends. She hoped that her adventure would lead her to her grandfather or maybe even the other world that Carlos spoke of, but she worried that it might lead them into more danger than she could imagine.

EIGHT

"Can you take us to the last place you saw him?" Michelle looked over her shoulder at Carlos. "Do you remember where that was?"

"Yes, I know it well." He frowned. "But it is dangerous there. Large creatures roam. Creatures far larger than you."

"We'll be careful." Michelle smiled. "I'm sure we'll be fine."

"I wouldn't be so sure." Carlos spoke softly. "I think there is something I should tell you."

"Yes?" Michelle swam closer to him. He still hung from Kira's hair. "What is it?"

"When I said I'd never seen your grandfather again, I didn't make myself clear. I have looked for him for many years, Michelle. I have found no sign of him." He looked into her eyes. "I fear he might have been taken by that whale—or some other creature."

"Taken?" Kira shivered. "Do you mean killed?"

"I hate to think it." Carlos shook his head. "But he and I were good friends. I do think that if he had survived, he would have found me to let me know that he was okay."

"Maybe he couldn't." Michelle's heart pounded. "Maybe he got lost."

"Your grandfather? Lost?" Carlos chuckled. "No, that's not possible. He knew the open sea better than any creature I've ever met. I don't think he could ever be lost."

"Then he is alive somewhere and we need to help him!" Michelle balled her hands into fists. "I know he is!"

"Okay, you may be right." Carlos nodded. "I will take you there. Keep swimming this way."

They did swim. They swam for hours before they all became too tired to swim any further.

"This is a good place to stop." Bea crawled off of Trina's shoulder and onto a flat rock that jutted out over a small open space. "Carlos and I will keep watch while you rest."

"Thank you." Michelle swam under the rock and stretched out in the sand. Soon Kira and Trina nestled in beside her.

She tried to imagine what her journey would have been like if she had made it alone. She couldn't even picture it. Having her two best friends beside her made everything seem better.

But as she started to drift off to sleep, she thought of her parents. How worried were they? What about her sisters? Did they know she was gone?

She guessed that they probably did. In fact, they were probably searching everywhere for her.

She had promised her friends she would go back home if she couldn't find her grandfather, but could she? The thought of how angry everyone would be made her sick to her stomach. How could she explain why she left?

Her thoughts shifted to the other world Carlos had described. Was it possible that he was telling the truth? Could there be another place? A world full of different creatures?

The thought thrilled her. She wanted more than anything to learn about it. But first, she had a mission to complete. If her grandfather was out there somewhere all alone, she wanted to find him. Maybe he could explain to her why her parents and the rest of the mermaid world had kept so many secrets.

When she woke up, it surprised her. She hadn't realized that she'd fallen asleep. Yet she had the sense that quite a bit of time had passed. Kira and Trina were still asleep. So was Bea, curled up on Trina's shoulder. But Carlos guarded them all.

"Carlos?" She swam out to him. "Did I sleep a long time?"

"A very long time." He smiled. "You must have been tired."

"I was." She looked around in the water. "Was it quiet?"

"Yes, a little too quiet." He tipped his head toward the others. "We should wake them and be on our way."

"Why do you think it's too quiet?" She peered through the water.

"When there aren't many creatures around, there's usually a reason." He scuttled back toward the sleeping mermaids. "Let's go! Wake up, little fish!"

"Fish?" Kira woke up with a start. "Did you just call me a fish?"

"I'm sure he meant it in a nice way." Trina stretched her arms out above her head.

"How could calling me a fish be nice?" Kira crossed her arms.

"I meant no offense." Carlos laughed. "Just that you swim like fish, so I think of you as fish."

"Well I am most certainly not a fish!" Kira frowned as she swam out to join Michelle.

"We're a little bit like fish." Michelle shrugged. "We have the tails, the scales, and the gills."

"Ugh, not you too!" Kira spun through the water in a swift and fancy twirl. "Can fish do that?"

"Not any that I've seen." Carlos clacked his claws. "Very nice!"

"Thank you. So, remember, I'm a mermaid, not a fish!"

"I'll remember, but there's no time to argue! We must move on my mermaid friends—and quickly!"

"Why?" Trina looked around. "Everything looks peaceful."

"Yes, it does look peaceful, that's the problem!" He looked around quickly, then waved his claws through the water. "Hurry! We must go!"

"Oh dear, we might be too late." Bea slid up along Trina's shoulder until she reached the top of her head. "Something is casting a very big shadow.

Michelle looked up in time to see a dark shadow glide over the top of them. It was larger than any shadow she'd ever seen.

"Is that what I think it is?" Kira ducked behind Michelle.

"It might be." Trina huddled close as well. "I've heard stories about enormous sharks, but I'd hoped that they were made up to keep us close to home."

"I'm sorry to tell you that they're not just stories." Carlos grabbed onto Kira's hair. "We need to get out of here and fast. Hopefully the shark didn't spot us!"

"I'm pretty sure it did!" Trina shrieked as the water began to rumble all around them. "Swim faster! Faster!"

NINE

Michelle's heart pounded as she swam as fast as she could. She didn't dare to look back, but she could imagine how huge and hungry the shark might be. Would he go after all of them or just one?

She realized that if she didn't do something, they might all become dinner. Maybe she wasn't ready to be a princess, but that didn't mean that it wasn't her job to protect her people.

She glanced over at each of her friends, then she suddenly changed direction.

"Keep swimming!" she shouted to them. "I'll distract the shark!"

She swam straight toward the shark, which was far larger than she'd even imagined. It made her dizzy with fear to stare at his wide mouth as he cut through the water in her direction.

"Michelle!" Trina shouted. "Get away from it!"

"It's too late!" Kira grabbed Trina's arm. "We have to keep going, it's what she wants us to do!"

"But she'll never make it!" Trina fought against Kira's grip.

"If anyone can, it's Michelle." Kira tugged her forward. "We can't let Carlos and Bea get eaten, not after Michelle has done this to protect all of us."

Michelle did her best not to think about the danger she'd put herself in. As long as her friends made it out safe, she would be happy. But the shark that barreled toward her was hard to ignore.

She ducked off to the side and tried to swim around him. As she did, she felt the ripple of the water that splashed off of his body. He moved so fast that he created his own current, a current that she found herself caught up in.

As she tumbled in the force of the water, she realized that she wouldn't be able to escape.

Just as she was ready to surrender, a shrill sound rang through her ears. It was so loud and so overpowering that she clutched at her ears in an attempt to escape it. As she twisted and covered her ears, the shark thrashed and rolled through the water.

He seemed to be just as bothered by the sound as she was. It made the water feel electrified.

Her skin prickled and her teeth chattered.

The shark lunged toward her, then sank to the sand below. He rolled there for a few seconds, then bolted off in the opposite direction.

Michelle stared after him as her ears continued to ring. She looked in the direction her friends had swum in, but they were gone. As she rubbed her ears, she realized she was safe. The shark had been scared off by the sound.

Still a little dizzy from the ringing, she sank down to the sand for a rest.

"Michelle!" Trina shouted.

"Michelle, where are you?" Kira shouted.

"I'm here!" Michelle waved her hand through the water. "The shark is gone, I'm here!"

"Oh, Michelle!" Trina swam toward her with Kira right behind. As they hugged, all three friends laughed with relief.

"How did you escape?" Carlos stared at her.

"That was the biggest shark I've ever seen." Bea crept out from under Trina's hair.

"I didn't escape." Michelle shook her head. "Something saved me. It was this sound—a sound like nothing I've ever heard before." She turned to look through the water. "I think it came from that way." She pointed toward a faint glow in the distance.

As she stared, she saw something move in the water.

"Look!" Michelle pointed to a figure ahead of them. "It's a mermaid!"

"Are you sure?" Trina tilted her head to the side. "Maybe it's just a big fish?"

"It's not a big fish!" Michelle huffed, then swam forward.

The closer she came to the figure, the more excited she became.

The mermaid, however, managed to swim just faster than her. If she noticed Michelle following her, she didn't turn back to see who it was. She had a faint glow around her and something strapped over her shoulder—something that Michelle had never seen before.

"Wait! Please!" She swam as fast as she could. "Please stop!"

The mermaid suddenly turned to face her and that's when Michelle realized that it was a merman, not a mermaid.

His long white hair flowed around his head. His eyes glowed a mixture of green and black as the deepest waters she'd ever seen. They reminded her of her mother's eyes.

"Grandfather?" She stared at him.

"You shouldn't be here." He stared back at her.

"I've been looking for you." She shook her head. "I thought you might need my help."

"You thought I might need your help?" He chuckled. "Little princess, all I need is for you to be safe."

"I'm not a princess!" Michelle crossed her arms. "Not yet at least. I wanted to explore. I didn't want to be trapped in the Coral Palace."

"Trapped in the Coral Palace? What do you mean?" He looked up as the others gathered close. "What are the three of you doing so far away from home? Carlos, is that you?"

"It's me!" Carlos waved as he hung from Kira's hair. "Good to see you again, old friend!"

"You too." The merman smiled. "I thought that whale got you."

"I thought he got *you*!" Carlos chuckled. "I'm so glad to see that he didn't."

"Was it you that saved me from that shark, Grandfather?" Michelle swam closer to him.

"It wasn't me exactly, but a special tool I was given." He patted the small square box that hung from his shoulder. "It emits a sound that the sharks don't like. It's kept me safe a few times and I'm glad I had it to keep you safe." He frowned. "This part of the sea isn't safe for you."

"I just want to have adventures and explore—like you!" She smiled. "Can't I stay with you? Please?"

"No, darling." He wrapped an arm around her. "What I am doing, you can't help me with. I've made some terrible mistakes and now I'm trying to fix them."

"Mistakes? What kind of mistakes?"

"Because of me, the human world suspects that mermaids exist. I've been trying to protect the mermaid world from being discovered ever since." He hung his head. "There isn't a day that goes by that I don't wish I had stayed in the Coral Palace."

TEN

"Then why don't you come back with us?" Michelle took her grandfather's hand. "Mother misses you so much."

"I'm sure that she does. I'm sorry that I was never able to tell her that I'm safe. But now you can be the one to tell her." He pulled a chain of gems from around his neck.

"Take this treasure back to your mother." He handed her the string of gems. "She will know what to do with it."

"But Grandfather, I don't want to go back." She drew back from the gems. "I don't care about treasure. I want to explore. I want to see what you've seen—and more."

"Michelle, it is far too dangerous." He looked up at the water that sparkled with the sunlight that drifted down through it. It created the glow all around him. "I know it is tempting. It all looks so beautiful." He looked back at her. "But the truth is, the world up there—the world of the humans—it's a cruel and terrifying place. Our world is beautiful and peaceful and it's all we need. I made a terrible mistake by coming here, by contacting the humans, and now I have to try to fix it by keeping them away from our world. That is my job now and I have to keep doing it."

"But Grandfather—"

He lifted the string of gems and hung it around her neck. "Now your job is to get safely back home and give this to your mother. Tell her that you've seen me, tell her that I am doing my best to protect everyone." He shook his head. "Tell her that I'm sorry that I've caused this danger to spread." He looked straight into her eyes. "Whether or not you want to be a princess, little one, you are a princess. It is your job to keep the mermaid world and the Coral Palace safe. Can I count on you to do that?"

"It can't be so terrible." Michelle frowned. "I've seen a giant squid, an octopus, and an enormous shark. What could be more terrible than that?"

"It is far more terrible than any of those things." He touched her cheek. "There was a time when I believed that the human world and the mermaid world should communicate. But now I know how wrong I was. Please, promise me that you will do your best to protect our world."

"I promise." Michelle bit into her lip. She wanted to ask a million questions, but she knew that he wouldn't answer them. "I'll go back and I'll give my mother these gems."

"Good." He smiled as he looked at her. "It is good to know that there is such a brave young princess guarding the Coral Palace in my absence. And you both will help her?" He looked at Kira, then Trina.

"We will." Kira nodded. She took Michelle's hand. "It's time to go home now."

"But we can't." Michelle glanced over her shoulder. "We don't know the way."

"The gems will guide you." Her grandfather pointed to the necklace. "They will glow as you go in the right direction. Just follow their glow."

"I will." Michelle clutched the gems. "I wish I could stay with you."

"One day I will tell you of all my adventures, but right now, your most important job is to be crowned a princess, so that you can keep our family and our world safe." He touched the top of her head. "Be safe, my granddaughter, and journey home swiftly. Your journey may be coming to an end, but your adventure is just beginning."

Swimming away from her grandfather was the hardest thing Michelle ever had to do.

As she swam, the gems on the necklace glowed. If she went in the wrong direction, the glow faded until she was going in the right direction again. She was curious about how they worked and sad that she had to leave her grandfather behind. But she was very excited to tell her mother about her discovery.

When they arrived at the Coral Palace, guards rushed toward them.

"It's the princess!" one of them shouted. "She's returned!"

Soon the shout was repeated in many different voices in many different directions.

Michelle braced herself as she swam into the Coral Palace. Would her mother be angry? Had she missed her chance to be crowned?

"Michelle!" Her mother swam toward her, her arms spread wide. "Oh, Michelle! You are safe!" She looked past her at Kira and Trina. "You're all safe! What a joyous day!"

"I'm sorry, Mother, I know I shouldn't have left. But I felt I had no choice. I wanted an adventure." She lifted the gems from around her neck. "I found Grandfather and he asked me to bring these to you."

"You what?" Her mother's eyes widened. "You found him?" As she took the gems, her hands trembled. "Is he well?"

"Yes. He said that he has a job to do—to protect the mermaid world. He can't come back yet, but he said that you would know what to do with these. They aren't sea gems, are they?"

"No, they're not." Her mother stared at them. "I suppose it's time I told you the truth. Will you excuse us please, Kira and Trina? I know that your families are waiting to see you."

"Yes, of course." Trina started to back away.

"Oh, Trina dear, you have something on your shoulder!" The queen's eyes widened.

"This is Bea." Trina smiled. "A friend."

"And I'm Carlos!" The lobster swung from Kira's hair and attempted to bow slightly. "Pleasure to meet you, my queen!"

"Oh my!"

"Mother, they kept us safe and helped us on our journey. Can't they stay?" Michelle looked into her eyes.

"Of course they can. They are welcome. Now, Michelle, come with me."

Michelle took her mother's hand as she led her through the Coral Palace. They traveled down corridors that she'd never seen before, until they reached a space deep under the sand.

"Your grandfather began collecting things when he was a young merman." She pulled back thick piles of seaweed. "He knew they were not of our world. He saved them here. He hoped that one day he would be able to learn more about the human world." She looked over at Michelle. "Since his disappearance, we all thought it would be better if we never mentioned the other world. We thought it would keep you safer." She moved aside to give Michelle a view of the space.

It was filled with strange items of all shapes and sizes, things that Michelle knew didn't belong in the sea.

"Mother! I had no idea this was here." She began to swim forward.

"Don't, Michelle. It is forbidden." She let the seaweed fall back into place. "I am only showing you now, so that you can help me protect the others. Your grandfather thought the humans would want to work with us to protect the sea, but I guess that is not what happened."

"No. He said the human world was a terrible place." She frowned. "Can that really be true?"

"If he says it is, then it is as I feared." She clutched the gems tightly in her hand. "It's time for your crowning, Michelle. I hope now you know just how important it is for you to protect our world."

"I do."

Michelle followed her mother back to the throne room.

As all the mermaids gathered, including her father, sisters, and friends, she finally understood what it meant to be a princess. But she also knew that guarding the palace would never be enough for her.

As the crown was placed on her head she smiled at her friends. Now she understood that she had a job to do, that she would have to do much more to protect her world.

She thought of her grandfather and the adventures she still wanted to have and somehow she knew that one day her dreams would come true. One day, she'd see with her own eyes this other world that existed. One day, her grandfather would come back to Eldoris to live with them again in the Coral Palace.

BOOK 2: TRINA

CHAPTER 1

Trina turned over in her shell and watched as tiny bubbles floated through the water beside her. Bubbles fascinated her. They were like their own little worlds inside the water. She often wondered what it would be like to be inside of one.

Did they have secrets too?

Ever since her friend Michelle's crowning, secrets were the only things Trina could think about—the secrets that she had to keep and the secrets that she had yet to discover.

Some time had passed since her adventure into the deep sea with Michelle and Kira. They'd met a few friends and found Michelle's grandfather.

He held the biggest secret of all. There was another world. Not inside of a bubble—not as far as she knew—but above the water.

For all of her ten years, Trina had believed—like most of the other mermaids in Eldoris—that the idea of a world above the water was just a fantasy. She'd never come close enough to the top of the water to imagine that it could be real.

From a very young age, mermaids were taught to always

swim down when possible. Never risk getting too close to the sparkling sunlight that made the water glow.

Now, seeing what was above the water was all Trina could think about.

She sat up in her shell and looked through the water at the other slumbering figures around her.

Since Michelle had moved into the Coral Palace, she and Kira had moved in as well to be her attendants. Trina shared a sleeping space with Kira and many other mermaids that worked there. It was the safest place they could be, but to Trina, it had become a nightmare.

She couldn't sleep. She couldn't focus on anything other than the discoveries she'd made on her adventure with Kira and Michelle.

As she swam quietly through the water, she hoped that she wouldn't wake anyone. She was just about out the door when a tiny voice drew her attention.

"Where are you going, Trina?" A sea slug crawled along the rocky wall of the sleeping space.

"Nowhere, Bea—just for a swim," Trina whispered to her. "Go back to sleep."

"I'm not sleepy." The sea slug raised her head and smiled. "I'll go with you."

"It's better if you don't." Trina frowned. "Just stay here."

"Trina." Bea crawled up along her fingers and onto her arm. "Are you looking for it again? I thought you learned your lesson about that."

"I know it has to be here somewhere. I heard Michelle speaking to her mother about it. I just want to see for myself." Trina stared at the small creature. "You know why I can't let it go."

"I know that you learned too much on our adventure. I know that you haven't been sleeping. But that's no excuse for breaking the rules of the Coral Palace. The queen would not be pleased."

"I don't plan to get caught." Trina smiled and raised an eyebrow. "Unless a noisy sea slug like yourself gets me into trouble."

"I won't say a word." Bea crawled up her arm and onto her shoulder. "But I'm going with you."

Trina sighed. She knew better than to argue with Bea. For such a small creature, Bea was quite stubborn.

She swam through the corridors of the Coral Palace.

Over the past few nights, Trina had been searching for a room that she'd heard Michelle talk about with her mother—a room that held proof of this other world. Trina wanted to see it for herself. She wanted to know once and for all if there really was another world.

She thought about the nearly invisible string that Kira had been tangled in on their adventure. It was like nothing she'd ever seen before. Carlos, a lobster who'd rescued Kira, had called it fishing line. But was he right? Or was that just another made-up story?

After believing that the ocean was the only world that existed for so long, she needed proof to change her mind. That proof, she believed, was in the secret room.

She'd asked Michelle about it, but she had refused to say a word. As a princess of Eldoris, it was Michelle's job to protect all the mermaids and that meant following the rules.

Michelle had become quite the rule follower.

Trina swam down through a corridor. It led to another corridor that she had yet to explore. The deeper she went, the more confusing the many corridors became. It was like a maze and Trina easily got turned around.

Just as she convinced herself that she'd already been in the same corridor three times, she came across a doorway that was covered in thick seaweed.

"This is new." She ran her fingertips along the seaweed. "I've never seen this before."

"Trina, maybe we should go back." Bea crept along Trina's neck to her other shoulder. "If you're caught somewhere you shouldn't be, you might get kicked out of the palace. Michelle wouldn't be happy about that."

"No, she wouldn't." Trina frowned. "But I can't turn back now, Bea. I think this is it. I think I've finally found it!"

"Once you look inside, you'll never be able to look away again," Bea whispered. "You might find something that you wish you hadn't."

"Maybe." Trina wrapped her fingers around a big chunk of the seaweed. "But at least I'll know the truth—finally. I can't keep lying awake at night wondering what's real and what isn't. I have to know if there's another world out there as Michelle's grandfather claimed—as Carlos says there is—and as our queen wants us to believe there isn't." She glanced over at Bea. "You don't have to stay with me. If I get caught, you get caught too."

"I'm not going anywhere." Bea nestled close to Trina's hair. "If you're going to look, you'd better look fast before someone notices that you're missing."

"This is it." Trina narrowed her eyes, then pulled back the thick seaweed.

CHAPTER 2

Inside the hidden room, the water was murky and dark.

Trina expected something different. Maybe even something magical. She expected shimmering light and something that would stun her. Instead, all she saw were faint shapes and glimmers of smooth surfaces.

"Let me help." Bea closed her eyes. A moment later, a blue glow began to emit from the sea slug. It was bright enough to light up the water around her.

"Bea! I didn't know that you could glow." Trina peered at the sea slug. "You have your secrets too, don't you?"

"I guess I do." Bea glowed brighter. "Hurry and have a look before someone notices the glow."

"Wow." Trina's eyes swept over the variety of items piled up in the space. There were round hard things and long things that looked like stems but would only bend a little to the touch. She ran her hands over a long wooden item that was slim at the top and widened and flattened at the bottom. "What is this?" She noticed the grooves in the wood, as if something sharp had etched a cut into it.

"That is an oar," Carlos piped up from behind her.

"Carlos!" Trina dropped the oar. She spun around as it drifted down to the sand. Her eyes widened at the sight of the lobster who'd crept his way further into the room and the mermaid that swam in behind him. "Kira!"

"Trina." Kira crossed her arms as she looked at her friend. "What have you done?"

"I knew it!" Michelle swam in behind Kira. "Kira told me that you were sneaking around, but I didn't want to believe her. Tonight we followed you. How could you, Trina? You know this place is off limits."

"How could you keep it from me?" Trina placed her hands on her hips. "You may be a princess, but I thought you were still my best friend."

"I am!" Michelle swam closer to her. "I always will be! But you know better than to sneak around the palace. If my mother and father find out that you were here, you'll be in so much trouble."

"If?" Trina clasped her hands together. "Does that mean you're not going to tell them?"

"I should." Michelle frowned. "It's so important to protect all the mermaids from seeing these things."

"Why?" Trina shook her head. "If there really is another world, don't you think that everyone should know about it? It's only right."

"If the other mermaids knew about it, they'd be tempted to make contact with the other world." Michelle looked over the variety of items stored in the small space. "But we know the truth. We know that the human world is a terrible place and that any mermaid that tries to reach it would be in grave danger. It's my job to keep them all safe." She looked back at Trina. "Including you, Trina."

"We don't know that, though. Just because your grandfather said it was terrible—well, that isn't proof that it is." Trina picked up the oar from the sand and placed it back onto the rock it had rested on. “All of these things were created by humans, right?”

“As far as we know.” Michelle nodded.

“Well, how can they be so terrible if they can create such interesting and beautiful things?” She reached up and touched a collection of shiny circles that hung from invisible string. “I don’t know what it is, but it’s just so pretty.”

“That doesn’t mean they’re good.” Michelle frowned. “You heard what my grandfather had to say. He said contacting the humans was a big mistake.”

“Maybe.” Trina turned back to Michelle and Kira. “But how can we know for sure if we don’t investigate it ourselves?”

“You know I’m not allowed to leave the Coral Palace anymore. Once I was crowned, it became my duty to protect all the mermaids here.” Michelle touched the surface of a smooth, pink object. “Even if we wanted to find out more, I can’t leave.”

“That’s just it, though. How can we expect to protect Eldoris from the humans if we don’t know anything about them? In order to keep all the mermaids safe, we have to find out more. We have to know what we’re up against. Don’t you think?” Trina looked at Michelle. “How can we know how to protect Eldoris, if we don’t know who might be attacking it?”

“I suppose you’re right.” Michelle frowned. “I can speak to my parents about it. But until then, you need to stay out of this room. Understand?” She looked from Trina to Kira. “Both of you.”

“You don’t have to tell me twice.” Kira picked up a long metal pole. “Look at this thing. It must be a weapon of some kind.” She shivered as she let go of it. “No, I’m not the least bit interested in looking at any of this.”

“I’ll stay out, Michelle.” Trina grabbed a small tube-shaped item and snapped her fingers. She knew that it would be stowed away for her to access it whenever she needed it. She looked up at Michelle to see if she noticed. If she did, she didn't say a word about it.

"Everyone go back to sleep. I'll speak to my parents about it in the morning." Michelle looked over the contents of the room. "And remember, whether we agree with them or not, the rules are the rules. No one should know about this place. Not a word about it."

"Not a word." Trina nodded.

She followed the others out of the room.

As she swam away, she looked back over her shoulder. She wondered if she would ever be able to find her way back to the room again.

CHAPTER 3

"Can you hear anything?" Trina craned her neck and swam as close to the entrance of the throne room as she could.

"Nothing." Bea crept higher on the rocky wall. "I know they are talking, but it's too quiet for me to hear."

"This is crazy. We shouldn't be trying to listen in." Kira frowned, but inched closer to the entrance as well. "What if they don't agree with Michelle?"

"I know that I have to find out more. If Michelle can't come with me, then that is just how it will have to be." Trina shivered at the thought. She always tried to put on a brave face, but the truth was, the thought of venturing out into the deep sea again without her friends at her side frightened her. She thought about the giant squid, the octopus, and the enormous shark that she'd encountered the last time. If it hadn't been for the help of her friends, she might not have survived. Would she be able to survive if she was alone?

"Come in, Trina—and you too, Kira." The queen's voice rippled through the water.

Trina froze.

Kira's eyes widened.

"Yes. Yes, I know that you're both out there. Come in, we don't have time to play games."

"Should we?" Trina whispered to Kira.

"We don't have a choice." Kira whispered back. "We've been caught!"

"Let's go, you two!"

An entire wave sloshed toward them, pushed by the force of the queen's voice.

"Right here, my queen." Trina swam into the throne room and immediately bowed down to the queen. She felt Kira swim up beside her and do the same.

"And what do you have to say for yourselves?" The queen stared at them from her shell.

"I just wanted to make sure that Michelle was okay." Trina cleared her throat. "I mean, Princess Michelle." She winced. She was still getting used to that title.

"I see." The queen nodded. "And you as well, Kira?"

"Yes, my queen. Trina and I are both eager to do whatever we can to help Princess Michelle. I'm sorry if that made us a little too nosy." She frowned.

"It's quite alright. I'm glad to know that my daughter has two such loyal friends. We have discussed the matter and the king and I have decided that Princess Michelle's skills are better used in an effort to protect all of Eldoris. Because of that, we have agreed that she can take a journey into the open sea with the two of you. However, we will send a guard with you as well." She gestured to a merman who floated not far from the royal shells. "Bernard will keep the three of you safe. You are to listen to whatever he tells you to do. Understand?"

Trina stared at Bernard. She didn't know him well, but she knew that he wasn't much older than they were. Would he really be any help? She hoped that, at the very least, he wouldn't make things more difficult.

A wave of relief washed over her as she realized that the king and queen had just given them permission to explore. She hadn't thought that would ever happen. Now that it had, her heart pounded harder than ever. What had she gotten herself into? Could she really handle exploring the deep sea in search of more information about the human world?

"I understand, my queen." Trina gave a deep bow to the queen and king. Then she smiled at Michelle as she swam down from her shell.

"We will leave in a few hours, once we've had time to gather the supplies that we need." Michelle swam over to both of them. "That is, if you'd both like to join me. I want you to know that you don't have to. This could be a dangerous journey and if either of you want to stay here, I understand."

"We will go with you." Kira smiled as she took Michelle's hand. "Trina and I would love to be at your side."

"Yes, we would." Trina smiled as well. She did her best to ignore the nervous beat of her heart. She had to be strong. This was her idea, after all.

"Be ready in exactly two hours," Bernard instructed them as he swam past with a snap of his tail.

Trina watched him swim swiftly away. It was hard for her to believe that she would be stuck exploring with him—she already didn't like his bossy nature—but she did think it was best to have some added protection on their journey.

"What's his problem?" Kira scrunched up her nose. "He seems a little tense."

"I think maybe we all need to be a little more tense about this." Michelle swam beside them. "We're thinking of this as an adventure, but the truth is, the closer we get to the human world, the more danger we'll be in."

"At least, that's what we believe." Trina looked at her friends. "We don't know that it's true."

"We only have evidence that it is." Michelle shook her head. "We have to assume that they are dangerous."

"I wonder if they would think the same thing about us." Trina raised an eyebrow. "Do you think we're like a story to them? Just a myth that they can't be sure is true? Something wonderful and scary at the same time?"

"Maybe." Kira tipped her head from side to side. "It's hard to imagine that anyone could find us scary."

"Trust me, it's not that hard." Bea crawled along the back of Trina's neck. "You are the strangest creatures I have ever seen."

"This from a glow-in-the-dark sea slug?" Trina laughed.

"I suppose we all seem a little strange at first." Bea smiled.

CHAPTER 4

While the others prepared for the journey, Trina swam off on her own. She even left Bea inside the palace.

Once she was sure that she was alone, she snapped her fingers. The metal tube landed in her hand out of nothingness. She turned it over in her hands.

It was longer than her hand—just about as long as her forearm. It started out narrow and gradually got a little wider at the other end. She noticed that both ends were opened but covered in something that looked like sea glass—but it was far more clear than any sea glass she'd ever seen.

She shook it. It didn't make a sound. She turned it over in her hands again. It felt as if it was hollow. She wondered if she could see right through it from end to end. She put the narrow end up to her eye and pointed the other end away from her.

"Ah!" She dropped the tube and swam backwards at the sight of a giant slug that looked large enough to consume her in one bite.

"Trina? Are you okay?" Bea swam closer to her.

Trina blinked, then stared at the sea slug. She was just as tiny as she'd always been.

"How did you do that?" She narrowed her eyes.

"Do what?" Bea swam down through the water and landed on the metal tube that had settled in the sand. "I knew you took something from that room. You really shouldn't have done that, Trina."

"You were just huge!" Trina crossed her arms. "You never told me that you could make yourself giant."

"What are you talking about?" Bea stared up at her. "I can't make myself any bigger than I am." She looked down at the tube. "What is this thing?" She crawled down to the end of it and peered through the small end. The large end was pointed in Trina's direction.

Trina swam down toward it.

"Ah!" Bea somersaulted through the water and wriggled in pure panic. "Stay back, beast!"

"Bea? It's just me." Trina stared at her.

"No, it's a giant version of you!" Bea opened one eye and looked at her. "Oh good, you're you again."

"I didn't change." Trina frowned. She stared at the metal tube. "It must be this thing. That must be what is making things look bigger." She snatched it up from the sand. "Bea, stay right there."

Trina pointed the large end of the tube at Bea, then looked through it. She shuddered at the sight of the giant slug. Then she lowered the tube. Bea shrank back down into an adorable little sea slug.

"This thing must be magic!" Trina smiled as she looked it over. "It can make things bigger." She pursed her lips. "Actually, it can make them appear bigger. We don't really change sizes, it just looks like we do."

"What would be the point of that?" Bea floated through the water.

"I'm not sure." She put the tube up to her eye again and looked in the direction of the Coral Palace.

Suddenly, Michelle, Kira, and Bernard were right in front of her. Her heart raced as she realized that she'd been caught with an item from the secret room.

She dropped it quickly. When she did, the other mermaids vanished. Confused, she peered through the water. In the distance, she could see faint outlines of her friends and Bernard. Had they been that far away the whole time?

She snapped her fingers so that the tube would disappear. "Maybe it's to help things that are far away seem closer? No time to think about it now, it looks like everyone is ready to go."

Bea climbed onto her shoulder. Trina swam toward the others.

"There is no reason for him to come with us." Bernard crossed his arms as he stared at Carlos. "He'll just slow us down."

"He rides with me." Kira frowned. "Carlos is coming with us."

"I am in charge here and I was instructed to escort the three of you, not a lobster and certainly not that." He pointed at Bea.

"Excuse me?" Bea reared up on Trina's shoulder.

"They're going." Trina looked straight at Bernard. "They both helped us on our last journey. Carlos knows more about the human world than any of us do. Bea can glow in the dark and light our way in dark places."

"She's right, I think it would be best if they came along." Michelle met his eyes. "Are you going to question me?"

"No, princess." Bernard frowned. "Then we should get going. We've already wasted enough time." He swam off ahead of them.

"That's the wrong way!" Carlos called out.

"This is going to be a very long journey." Kira shook her head.

Trina noticed a necklace of gems around Michelle's neck.

"Your mother let you take it?" She smiled.

"Yes, she did—so we won't get lost. Which, with Bernard along, is going to be very important." She laughed as he swam back toward them.

"This way." Carlos pointed his claw through the water. "It will get us closer to where the humans can be seen."

"Stay together." Bernard cleared his throat, then swam in the direction that Carlos pointed.

As Trina swam behind the group, she thought about the metal tube. Someone had created that. It wasn't something that grew, it wasn't made out of natural materials. Someone had invented it, designed it, and then built it. She guessed that the being who created it had to have a brilliant mind. It wasn't a weapon, it was a tool.

Could a human who invented something so wonderful really be all bad?

She guessed that they would find out soon enough. The idea terrified her and thrilled her at the same time.

CHAPTER 5

Lost in thought, Trina didn't realize that she'd drifted a bit far behind the others. She wondered if there would be a moment when she would have to confess to Michelle that she'd stolen something from the secret room. Maybe she could return the tube to the room before anyone found out.

"I said stay together!" Bernard swam up to her with a sharp snap of his tail.

The motion sent a ripple of water right into her face.

"Bernard!" She frowned as she ducked. "Relax!"

"It's a simple instruction. Stay with the group. If you can't keep up, then there's still time for you to turn back." He stared at her. "I won't let anyone put the princess in danger."

"I'm not putting her in danger." Trina glared at him, then swam up to her friends. It made her skin prickle to think of being stuck with Bernard for the whole journey. She wondered if there might be a way to leave him behind.

"Are you okay, Trina?" Michelle wrapped an arm around her shoulder.

"I'd be better if Bernard was a bit more friendly." She glanced at him as he swam up to the group.

"We should rest now." He pointed to a pile of rocks nearby. "Stay together. Don't be too loud. Don't make a lot of ripples."

"I'm not tired yet." Kira peered back through the water. "We haven't even gotten that far."

"It's better to rest before you're tired." Bernard sat down on one of the rocks. "Wearing yourself out to the point of exhaustion makes it harder to recover."

"Kira's right, we should go a little farther before we rest." Michelle looked at Carlos. "We still have a long way to go. Don't we, Carlos?"

"Yes, we do." Carlos peeked out from Kira's hair. "We must cross the deep sea before we get close to the shallow sea."

"All the more reason to rest now so that we'll have the strength to get through the entire journey." Bernard leaned back along the rock and looked up through the water. "This whole thing is pointless. We all know that humans aren't real."

"Is that what you think?" Carlos chuckled.

"I don't care what anyone says, no one is going to convince me that there's another world out there somewhere. It's ridiculous. My sister, Avery, talks the same nonsense. She insists that humans are real. But she doesn't have a clue. It's just a fantasy."

"They are real." Trina crossed her arms.

"Oh, really?" Bernard looked at her intently. "Have you seen one?"

"No." Trina frowned. "But that doesn't mean they're not real."

"Yes, actually it does. You can pretend they are, but it's all just imagination." Bernard rolled his eyes. "I just want to get through this and get back home to the real world."

"Why did you even come with us if you don't believe in our mission?" Michelle glared at him. "You should have told my mother how you felt."

"I don't question the queen." He shrugged. "Besides, I don't mind a journey and it's an important job to guard a princess."

"A princess that you think is a fool."

"I didn't say that." He swam up off of the rock. "Let's move on. We've had enough rest."

As they continued through the water, Trina swam up beside Michelle. "Are you sure about this?" She looked over at her friend. "Bernard might make things difficult."

"Just ignore him. The important thing is that my parents trusted us all enough to let us take this journey. We don't want to let them down, do we?"

"No, you're right." Trina smiled at the thought. It *was* nice to be trusted with such a big responsibility. "Do you think we'll actually see a human this time?"

"Enough talking!" Bernard snapped. "You're going to draw the attention of a predator."

"Enough, Bernard!" Michelle put her hands on her hips as she stared at him. "You're here to protect us, not to boss us around."

"You were told to listen to me." He stared back at her. "I'm not bossing you around, I'm making the best decisions I can to keep you safe."

"If you keep making these safe decisions, we're never going to get anywhere!" Trina plopped down on a rock and flipped her tail through the water. "We might as well be going in circles."

"I'm doing the best I can. The three of you don't even know where you're going." Bernard crossed his arms. "How am I supposed to protect you if I have no idea what we might run into?"

"Try to relax." Kira smiled at him. "There really isn't a reason to be so stressed. The open sea is perfectly safe most of the time."

"Until it's not." Bernard narrowed his eyes.

"Uh, excuse me." Carlos waved his claws through the water. "Hello? Down here!"

"Not now, Carlos." Kira waved her hand at him.

"Yes, now!" Carlos clacked his claws. "A little bit of that danger you two are arguing about is headed straight for us!"

"What is that?" Michelle swam back toward Trina.

"Stay back." Bernard turned to face the figure that grew closer and closer. "It's too far away, I can't tell what it is."

Trina's heart pounded. She knew that with the tube she would be able to see what it was. But if the others saw her using it, they would know that she'd taken it. She could be in a lot of trouble.

"I'm going to stop it from getting any closer." Bernard snapped his fingers. Suddenly there was a long thin pole in his hand with a very sharp tip.

"What is that?" Trina gulped.

"It's something the queen gave me to keep you all safe." He looked over at her. "Now be quiet so that I can aim!"

"But it's sharp! It will cut or even kill!" Kira swam closer to him.

"Stay back!" he barked at her.

Trina snapped her fingers as her heart raced. What if the figure that approached was just an innocent sea creature? She couldn't let Bernard hurt it. The metal tube landed in her hand. She put it up to her eye and looked through it in the direction of the figure.

"No!" she cried out. Then she slammed her shoulder into Bernard. "Don't throw that! It's your sister!"

CHAPTER 6

"What?" Bernard growled as he was knocked through the water.

"It's your sister! Avery!" Trina swam in front of him. "Don't you dare throw that weapon!"

"You're nuts! You can't tell who that is from here! Avery is back in Eldoris!"

"No, she's not." Trina held out the metal tube to him. "Look through this."

"Trina, what is that?" Michelle peered at it.

"Are you sure it's her?" Kira stared through the water. "I can't see at all from here."

"It's a tool. A human tool." Trina lowered her eyes. "It lets you see things that are far away."

"Like this?" Bernard put the large end up to his eye. "I can't see any better!"

"No, like this." Trina turned the tube around for him.

"Avery!" he shouted, then lowered the tube. He stared through the water. "How is that possible? What kind of magic is that?"

"I'm not sure." Trina clasped her hands together.

She felt Michelle's eyes on her.

Kira swam closer. "Where did you get that?" She eyed the tube. "Is it magic?"

"I don't think so. I don't know." Trina looked at Michelle. "I took it from the secret room. I know I shouldn't have, but I was so curious about it. I just wanted to see what it was for. Now that I've figured it out, I think it's pretty amazing."

"You shouldn't have taken that." Michelle crossed her arms. "You know it's forbidden."

"I know. I will tell the queen the truth when we get back. But for now, I think we should use it. It helped me see that it was Avery and not a predator coming toward us, after all."

"Let me see that." Michelle held her hand out to Bernard.

"Gladly. I'm going to go collect my sister." He swam off toward Avery.

Michelle and Kira took turns using the tube. "What do you think it's made out of?" Kira turned it over in her hands. "It's hard like a rock, but light."

"It's metal." Michelle tapped her fingertips on it. "My mother has taught me about a few of the items in the secret room, so that we can keep a lookout for other items like them. I'm not sure how it's made, but it's nothing that can be found in the sea."

"Oh dear, Bernard is pretty upset." Trina watched as he thrashed through the water while speaking to Avery.

"We should go over there." Michelle swam forward.

Trina and Kira followed after her. When they reached Bernard, his shouts made the water ripple around him.

"You are in so much trouble!" he shouted.

"I just wanted to come along." Avery frowned. "What's the big deal?"

"The big deal is that now I have to take you home!" Bernard pointed to the water ahead of them. "Let's go, start swimming!"

"Wait!" Michelle swam in front of him. "If we go back now,

we'll have lost so much time." Michelle looked at Avery. "I think we should let her join us."

"Join us? On this dangerous mission?" Bernard shook his head. "It's out of the question. She needs to go back home. Trina or Kira can take her."

"No." Avery glared at her brother. "I want to continue on with you. I know what this mission really is."

"What it really is?" Michelle raised an eyebrow. "What do you mean?"

"I mean that you're all here to hunt humans. If you find one, you might even hurt it!" She waved her hands through the air. "That's why I followed you—to make sure that you don't."

"That we don't hurt an imaginary creature?" Bernard chuckled.

"They're not imaginary." Avery looked from Michelle to Trina to Kira. "They're not, are they?"

"Whether or not they are imaginary, we would never cause them harm." Michelle swam over to Avery. "Not unless they tried to hurt us first. How do you know anything about them? Young mermaids aren't allowed to know about humans."

"I've overheard my father speaking about them."

"Avery!" Bernard barked. "Don't tell her that, you could get Father in a lot of trouble. Besides, everyone knows he's a little crazy."

"He's not crazy." Avery balled her hands into fists. "He has seen humans. He said so and I believe him."

"Your father has seen humans?" Trina swam over to her. "Are you sure?"

"Yes. He said that he saw a whole boat full of them." She snapped her fingers. A long flat rock appeared in the palm of one of her hands. "Do any of you even know what a boat is?"

"A boat?" Michelle peered at the rock. "That's a rock."

"My father kept this rock. He etched an image into it of

what he saw. He knew that no one would believe him. But this is a boat." She held out the rock to Michelle. "See?"

"What is a boat?" Kira tilted her head as she looked at the rock.

"My father says it's like a giant shell, but it floats on top of the water. Humans ride in it. That's how they can travel on the sea." She looked up at Michelle. "See how it has a curved bottom? That's how it floats."

"This is amazing." Michelle nodded.

"I've never seen anything like it." Trina stared at it. "I wonder if we could make something like that."

"Make a boat?" Bernard threw his hands up into the air. "For what? We're mermaids, we can't live outside of the water."

"I was just curious." Trina frowned. "Michelle is right, we've already wasted too much time. Avery should travel with us."

"Please, Bernard?" Avery looked at him with wide eyes.

"Fine, but only because I want you to see that there are no humans to be found. Hopefully you and Father can put this fantasy behind you once and for all." He snapped his tail sharply through the water as he swam off.

"Avery, you can swim with me." Kira smiled. "As long as you're not afraid of lobsters."

"Lobsters?" Avery swam closer to her.

"Hi!" Carlos popped out from beneath Kira's hair.

"Ah!" Avery swam backwards.

"Don't worry, I'm friendly!" Carlos shouted and clacked his claws.

CHAPTER 7

"Okay." Avery inched closer to Carlos. "If you say so."

"I do." He bowed his head to her. "Welcome to our adventure."

"Thank you." She smiled and bowed in return.

Trina swam ahead of Kira and Avery. She caught up with Michelle.

"I hope you're not too angry with me." She looked over at her.

"I'm not angry." Michelle frowned. "But you should be more careful. My parents have rules, and if you break them, you can get yourself into a lot of trouble."

"I know." She glanced back at Avery. "Do you think her father really saw what he says he saw?"

"He saw something and he etched a picture of it. That means there's something to see." Michelle lowered her voice. "I don't think he would lie about it. But Bernard is right. His father is known to have some strange ideas. It's hard to say."

"What if we don't find anything at all?" Trina stretched her arms out as she swam. "What if we came all this way for nothing?"

"We'll find something." Michelle narrowed her eyes. "I can feel it."

"I hope so." Trina smiled. "Want to race? We can make up for some time."

"I don't think Bernard would like that." Michelle looked over at Bernard, who slashed his arms angrily through the water and flipped his tail more than he needed to.

"All the more reason to do it." Trina grinned. She tapped Michelle lightly on the shoulder. "You're it!" She swam off through the water as fast as she could.

"Hey! That's cheating!" Michelle laughed and chased after her.

"Get back here, you two!" Bernard hollered.

"We're racing too!" Kira sung out. She and Avery began to swim as fast as they could.

"Slow down!" Carlos clung to Kira's hair.

"Unbelievable!" Bernard huffed as he tried to catch up to them.

"Ignore him." Avery rolled her eyes. "He thinks he's so important because he's twelve."

"I heard that, Avery!" he shouted.

"Is he always so bossy?" Kira whispered.

"Most of the time." Avery shook her head. "Mom says it's a phase. But I'm not so sure."

"He's just trying to do his job!" Michelle slowed down. "Maybe we shouldn't make it so hard on him."

"Oh, we're just having a little fun!" Trina grinned. "Maybe he'll loosen up a bit."

"That one?" Bea peered over Trina's shoulder. "I'm not sure that he knows what fun is."

"It's not so easy to figure out when you have responsibilities." Michelle swam a little faster—just fast enough to swat Trina on the back. "Got you!"

"You did!" Trina laughed and flipped through the water. After several turns, Bea squealed.

"So dizzy, so dizzy!" She slid right down Trina's arm and out into the water. "Ah, that's better."

"Sorry, Bea." Trina giggled. She glanced around at the rocks and coral around them. "It looks like we've gotten pretty far in a short time. I don't know about you, but I could use a rest."

"Me too," Kira moaned.

"That looks like a good spot." Michelle pointed to a rock archway. "Look at all the beautiful colors."

"Gorgeous!" Avery cooed. "I never get to see anything like this back home."

"Let's take a closer look." Kira swam toward the colorful plant-like creatures.

"Brr." Michelle shivered. "Is it just me or is the water a little colder all of a sudden?"

"It's not just you." Trina rubbed her arms. "We must have hit a cold spot."

"It feels pretty good after all that swimming." Kira floated through the archway on her back.

"The four of you are impossible!" Bernard huffed as he finally caught up to them. "What was the first rule I told you?"

"Stay together." Michelle smiled.

"Well, we are all together." Trina looked around at her friends, then back at Bernard. "So, I guess you're the one that was breaking that rule."

"You!" He jabbed a finger through the water as he pointed at her. "Just wait until I tell the queen about your human tool and the way you behaved. She will not like any of this!"

"Bernard, try to relax." Avery moaned. "We're just having fun."

"Too much fun can lead to big problems." He stretched out

on a rock. "Now rest, so we can be on our way soon. This cold water means that bad weather might be coming."

"How do you know?" Trina looked at him curiously.

"At home, we're so deep under water that we don't often feel the changes that happen to the sea when weather on the surface changes. But in these more shallow areas, the water can change a lot. The currents will get stronger and the water can get cold or even very warm. Sometimes it will even swirl."

"Swirl?" Kira looked up. "That sounds like fun."

"It's not fun if you're caught in it." Bernard frowned, then pointed up at the water above them. "See that glow? It's from sunlight. The more we can see it, the more shallow we are."

"Wow." Avery stared up at it. "It's beautiful. I want to touch it!"

"You can't touch it." Bernard rolled his eyes.

It was too late. Avery shot up through the water.

"Wait for me!" Trina swam after her. Michelle and Kira soon followed them both. "Ah the water is a little warmer here."

"Catch me if you can!" Michelle laughed as she slapped her tail through the water.

Trina chased after her.

Soon Kira and Avery had joined in as well.

Suddenly Bernard swam toward them. "Stop!" he shouted.

Trina laughed and dove down through the water toward Kira. "I'm going to get you!"

"Stop!" he shouted again. "Please! Listen to me!"

Something in his voice made Trina turn back to look at him. "What's wrong, Bernard?"

Her heart skipped a beat as he pointed above them. "Look!"

She saw a massive shadow. Larger than anything she'd ever seen before. Larger than any sea creature could ever be. It was high above them in the water. The shadow was thick enough to block out the thin tendrils of sunlight that had been drifting down through the water.

"Michelle! Kira! Look up!" Trina's eyes widened as she tried to take in the full length of the shadow. "What could it be?"

"It's a boat!" Avery smiled. "I know it is!"

CHAPTER 8

"A boat?" Bernard shrank back from the shadow. "It can't be."

"Look." Avery displayed her rock again. "It's the right shape." She started to swim upward. "If there's a boat, there must be humans on it. Let's go see!"

"No!" Bernard caught her by the ankle and pulled her back down. "Are you crazy?" He glared at her. "If they see us, we'll never see Eldoris again."

"He's right." Michelle swam up beside Avery. "The humans will want to hurt us. We have to be very careful."

"Maybe it's just a very bloated seal?" Kira swam up to the two of them.

"It's a boat." Trina gazed up at it. "It's a real boat." She swam a little higher than the others. "What do we do?"

"We stay away from it." Bernard crossed his arms.

"Isn't our job to find out more about the humans?" Trina met his eyes. "How can we find out more from down here?"

"Trina, we can't break the surface." Bernard looked at each mermaid in turn. "It is against the law to break the surface. It puts all of Eldoris at risk. All of you know this."

"Maybe you can't, but I can." Carlos floated away from Kira.

"I can't swim all the way to the top, though; someone will have to help me get there. Then you could toss me right up onto the boat."

"No!" Kira shook her head. "That's far too dangerous, Carlos."

"Danger is nothing to me." Carlos clacked his claws. "I may be small, but I am mighty."

"It's too risky." Michelle frowned. "I have no idea what might happen to you if you go up there."

"We all just need to take a minute to think about this." Kira began to swim back and forth. "We found a boat, which is amazing in itself."

"Right now it's just a shadow." Bernard peered up at it. "It could still be something else."

"It could be." Avery stared upward as well. "But it's not. The more time we waste talking about this, the less chance there is that we will get to see a human." She began to swim upward again. "I can only imagine how beautiful they are."

"Michelle's grandfather said they look like us, only with legs." Trina looked down at her long tail. "It must be so strange to have legs."

"Legs aren't the only things different about humans." Michelle caught up with Avery and wrapped an arm around her waist. "They live in an entirely different world. All we know about them is that they are likely monsters."

"You don't know that!" Avery pulled away from her.

"No, I don't know it for sure. But look at the weapon they created." She gestured to the sharp pole that Bernard had snapped into his hands. "What do you think that's for, Avery? Why would they need a tool like that? Its sharp blade is for killing."

"We're using it for protection." Trina swam up to Michelle and Avery. "Maybe that's what they use it for. Avery is right.

This is our one chance to see what humans are really like. We need to take it!" She looked over at Carlos. "If you really want to do this, Carlos, I will take you to the surface."

"Trina, no!" Michelle swam in front of her. "You can't go up there alone!"

"Then we'll go together." Trina stared into their eyes. "We have responsibilities, remember? Our job is to find out what we're up against. That means that we have to be brave and bend the rules sometimes."

"Break the law, you mean," Bernard growled. "If you two are going up there, then I'm coming with you to make sure that you're safe."

"Me too," Avery piped up.

"If Carlos is going, then I'm going with him." Kira swam up to them. "We'll be careful not to break the surface. We have Bernard to protect us."

"You have to promise not to hurt the humans!" Avery turned to face her brother. "Do you promise?"

"I promise that I will only use it to protect us." He locked his eyes to hers. "I will not let them hurt us."

"Calm down." Trina swam upward. "No one is going to get hurt."

As she neared the surface of the water, she noticed a shift in it. It seemed thinner, lighter almost. Her body felt lighter too. It was a strange sensation. The sunlight that poured through the surface of the water dazzled her.

As the others caught up, she watched the giant curved bottom of the boat glide past her. She reached her fingertips up through the water. It was so close, she thought she might be able to touch it.

"Don't!" Bea screeched in her ear. "You don't know where that thing has been!"

Trina jerked her hand back. Her heart skipped a beat. She

was fascinated by the texture and color of the bottom of the boat, not to mention its size.

"We must all be very careful." Michelle swam up beside Trina. "This is new to all of us."

"We can still turn back." Bernard looked up nervously as the boat continued to glide over them.

"We're not going anywhere." Avery smiled as she watched the boat. "I knew they were real!"

"Which means the monsters are real too." Michelle whispered. "The monsters that my grandfather described. They're right above us!"

Trina opened her mouth to disagree, but before she could, a noise louder than anything she'd ever heard shook her entire body. The water vibrated all around her.

CHAPTER 9

"What was that?" Trina stared up toward the surface of the water. Her stomach twisted with fear.

"I'm not sure." Michelle linked her arm around Kira's.

"I've never heard anything like it," Avery whispered.

"It's the bad weather." Bernard swam closer to the surface. "It's coming." He looked back down at them. "The water is getting darker. When storms come, the sunlight doesn't shine."

"Storms?" Michelle's eyes widened. "That sounds bad."

"It is." Bernard pointed down. "We need to get to deep water as fast as we can. Now!" He began to swim down.

"But the boat!" Avery swam upward instead. "I just want to have one look!"

"No!" Bernard shouted.

"Avery, we need to be safe. If Bernard says we have to go, then we should go." Michelle frowned.

"Bernard has been bossing us around for this entire journey." Trina crossed her arms. "This is our only chance to see this boat. If we swim to deep water, we'll never get back in time to see it again. It's going to pass us by."

"What's the point of seeing it, if we get swept up in a storm?" Kira shook her head. "It seems risky."

"Let's go!" Bernard growled. "There's no time to waste!"

Trina looked up at the bottom of the boat. She was so close that she could count the wooden planks. She wanted more than anything to see what was on it—who was on it. Would she ever have a chance like this again?

"I'm going!" She shot up through the water in the direction of the boat.

"Trina!" Michelle called after her.

"I'm right behind you!" Avery cried out and followed behind Trina.

As Trina got closer to the surface, she heard the loud sound again. Then suddenly the water was lit up by strange white light. She'd never been so scared.

As she stretched her arms above her head to swim upward, she felt a sensation that made her heart stop. Her fingertips pushed through the surface of the water and out into the open air.

Startled by the new sensation, she floated there.

"Trina, are you okay?" Avery swam up beside her but didn't reach up through the water.

"Trina, you broke the surface!" Michelle swam toward her.

"Trina, come back down!" Kira swam closer.

Bernard, with the sharp pole in his hand, swam past them. He floated just beneath the surface of the water.

"Listen to me, things are going to get rough. There will be big waves and lots of loud noises. We have to make sure that we stay together or we might get swept into completely different parts of the ocean." He held out an arm to Avery. "Link your arms together to make sure we don't get separated."

Avery shivered as another loud noise shook the water. She wrapped her arm around her brother's, then Michelle's.

Michelle wrapped her arm around Kira's.

Kira turned to grab hold of Trina's arm, but Trina's fingertips were still above the surface of the water.

"It feels so strange." Trina whispered. She reached her hand a little further out of the water.

"Trina, not too far! What if someone sees you?" Michelle frowned.

"It's time for me to do my part." Carlos let go of Kira's hair and swam toward Trina. "Lift me above the water, I can do the rest."

Trina wanted to know about the humans so badly. She knew that Carlos would learn so much if she gave him the chance. But as another loud sound carried through the water and more white light flashed, a sick feeling in her stomach made her pull her hand back.

"No, Carlos." She looked straight at him. "It's not safe. You're more important than finding out about the humans."

"I am?" Carlos floated in front of her. "Are you sure? Because no one has ever told me I'm important before."

"You're important to me, Carlos." Trina smiled.

"To all of us," Kira added.

"Now can we swim down to safety, please?" Bernard rolled his eyes.

"Yes, let's go." Trina looked over at Avery. "I know how curious you are, but now isn't the time."

"It might be the only chance we get!" Avery moaned.

"I know." Trina nodded. "It's so hard to swim away, but we're not prepared to handle a storm and Bernard is the only one that seems to understand this bad weather. He might have been bossy from the get-go, but that doesn't mean that he's not right."

"Oh no!" Bernard pointed up at the bottom of the boat. "Something's not right!"

The bottom of the boat tilted one way and then the other. Then it tilted very hard in their direction.

"It's going to tip over!" Avery cried out. "It's going to sink down into the sea!"

"Into us!" Michelle gulped. "Everyone swim away from it! As fast as you can!"

Trina couldn't look away from the shifting boat. She couldn't get her body to move. Her tail wouldn't flick. Her arms wouldn't swim. She couldn't think of what to do to get herself to safety. She was aware that all her friends had begun to swim as fast as they could. But she couldn't join them.

"Trina!" Bea squeaked from her shoulder. "You have to swim!"

Bernard glanced back and spotted Trina still near the surface of the water. He swam straight for her.

"Trina! I'll save you!"

CHAPTER 10

When Bernard's arms wrapped around Trina's waist, she could finally move again.

She swam toward her friends with Bernard at her side. Before she could get far, she heard a loud splash. She looked up in time to see a figure. It descended through the water. It had arms, hair, and a head just like hers. But where its tail should have been were two long legs.

"He's going to see us!" Bernard swam in front of Trina.

"Is that really what I think it is?" Trina couldn't look away from the human as he plummeted through the water.

"It's not a dolphin, if that's what you're asking!" Bernard huffed. "We have to get out of here before he sees us."

"Do you think he's okay?" Trina started to swim toward him.

"Trina! No!" He pulled her away from the still sinking human. "We have to go."

As Trina watched, the human began to swim. He stretched his arms up through the water and kicked his feet quickly. As she watched him get close to the surface, she was surprised by how well he could swim.

Just before he could break the surface, Bernard pulled her down through the water toward the others.

Her mind spun as she realized that she had just seen a human. A real human. Not an imaginary one, but a real one. She didn't know if she would ever see another human again, but she was certain that she would never forget that one.

As she began to swim deeper into the water, she caught sight of something that floated not far from her. She reached out and caught it in her hand. As she stared down at the little figure in her palm, her eyes widened.

"What is this?"

"Trina!" Michelle called out to her. "Get down here with the rest of us."

Trina closed her hand around the figure, then swam down toward her friends. Once she reached them, they all looked back up at the bottom of the ship. It continued to rock, but it no longer tilted. The water no longer vibrated and there were no more white flashes.

"Look." Bernard pointed to the surface of the water. "The sun is back."

Streams of sunlight pushed their way down through the water.

"It's true, it's really true." Avery clasped her hands together. "There is another world out there. Full of humans."

"Humans that would jump at the chance to hurt us if they knew we existed." Michelle frowned.

"That human was brave enough to survive the storm." Kira shrugged. "That's something new we've learned."

"It's not the only new thing we've learned." Trina opened her hand with her palm up. "I think the humans already know that we exist."

"Oh no!" Avery gulped. "Did they shrink a mermaid down into a tiny stone?" She poked at the mermaid figurine, which was attached to a metal loop and a single shiny piece of metal.

"It looks like that." Trina peered at the figure as well. "But I think it's made from something like metal. Only different." She poked at it too. "They did such a good job creating the tail, they must have a good idea of what we look like."

"This isn't good." Michelle began to swim back and forth. "If they know we're here—if they know we exist—that could mean that they're out looking for us. In fact, that boat might have been full of humans hunting for mermaids."

"Do you think he saw us?" Bernard frowned. "If he did, then we just confirmed that mermaids exist."

"I think he was too worried about getting back to the surface of the water to notice us."

"We can only hope that's the case." Michelle wrung her hands. "My mother is not going to be happy about this. Not at all." She looked at the figure again. "What is that attached to it?"

"I have no idea." Trina looked at the shiny object. "It feels like the same stuff that tube is made out of. Maybe it's also metal?"

"Maybe." Michelle looked back up through the water.

Trina looked up as well. She watched as the shadow of the boat coasted out of sight.

"We could have learned a lot more if we'd gone through with Carlos's plan." Trina looked over at the lobster, who was nestled back in Kira's hair.

"It wasn't safe." Bernard swam forward. "My job is to make sure that you all make it back to the Coral Palace safely."

"Now we know boats are real." Avery swam beside her brother. "We know that the human world is right above us. We know that they know about us." She looked back at Trina. "It changes a lot, don't you think?"

"Yes, it does." Trina held the figure tightly in her hand.

"It changes everything." Michelle swam beside Trina. "If the humans know about us—if they know what we look like—then that means we have been seen by more than one human. Which means that some of us have been breaking the law."

"But who?" Kira shook her head. "I can't imagine that any of us would do that."

"Your grandfather for one." Bernard snapped his tail. "He broke the law, that's for sure."

"He didn't break the law. He just followed his instincts." Michelle frowned. "Besides, even if he was seen, it couldn't have been by too many humans. He's very careful."

"We're going to have a big task in front of us when we get back home." Kira narrowed her eyes. "Before we learn anything more about these humans, we need to find out more about the mermaids around us. If some of them are sneaking up to the surface, then we have to find out who and put a stop to it." She shivered. "I've never seen anything so unnerving before. Did you see those legs? The way he swam?" She closed her eyes. "It was scary."

"Scary?" Avery twirled through the water as she smiled. "I thought he was beautiful. Maybe not as graceful as we are, but still beautiful."

"Don't get any ideas, Avery." Bernard looked at his sister. "Kira is right. Humans are frightening. Now that I know they're real, I can only imagine the kind of destruction they probably cause." He snapped his fingers and the long sharp pole appeared in his hands. "Remember, this was created by a human." He pointed to the sharp blade at the end of the pole. "Who do you think that is designed to hurt?"

Trina stared at the blade as it glimmered in the water.

Was Bernard right? If humans were hunting mermaids, then Eldoris was in grave danger. If the human that fell into the water had seen her, then there was a good chance he'd be back. What would happen if they were discovered?

But somewhere deep inside, Trina had to wonder if humans could really be all bad. Somehow she just didn't believe it could be the case.

BOOK 3: KIRA

CHAPTER 1

Kira picked up a long piece of material. It was brightly colored and soft enough to wrap around her hand. It had different shapes on it. As she looked up from it to the rest of the collection in the room, she frowned. She'd spent hours going through all the items from the human world and she didn't feel as if she knew anything more than when she'd started. It seemed to her that humans liked to create, but why?

She didn't know the purpose of any of it. It was like peeking into another universe and trying to piece together every tiny bit of it.

"Are you still in here?" Avery poked her head through the thick seaweed and into the room. "Michelle and Trina have been looking for you."

"They have?" Kira looked over at her. "I guess I didn't realize how long I've been in here." She let the cloth in her hand float away. "All of this is just so fascinating. Sometimes I picture a human creating one of these things and I try to imagine what they might be thinking. Why all the color? Why the different materials?"

"I think about that too." Avery swam in beside her. "They're so creative. They've invented so many things. I'd just love to meet one and find out more about them."

"Don't say that." Kira narrowed her eyes. "Don't ever say that, Avery. Meeting a human would be far too dangerous."

"We don't know that." Avery frowned. "They could be thoughtful and curious, just like us."

"They are hunters." Kira pointed to the various weapons that had been collected in the room. "Those aren't tools of creativity, they are tools of destruction."

"We think." Avery swam up to one of the bladed tools and peered at it. "Maybe their world is just so dangerous that they need these weapons."

"If that's the case, then it's definitely not a world we want to be part of, right?" Kira shook her head. "I want to learn more about the human world, because I want to make sure that we can protect ourselves from it. I keep thinking about the human that fell into the water. Did he see Trina? Did he see Bernard? We weren't that far from home. What if he comes back looking for us?"

"Humans stay on land most of the time." Avery swam back to Kira's side. "My father says he doesn't think they can survive under water."

"Maybe not. But what do you think this is for?" She picked up a round object with a glass circle in the front.

"I don't know. Some kind of container? Like a shell?" Avery tipped her head to the side.

"Or something like this." Kira slid the object over the top of her head until it rested on her shoulders. "It's a little big, I think."

"What? I can't hear you." Avery stared at her. "It's some kind of protection for their heads?"

Kira pulled the object off of her head and let it float away. "No, I think it's something to help them under water. I'm not sure how yet, but I'm pretty sure the humans are interested in exploring the sea. Why else would they build boats? Why else would they create tools that end up in the ocean?" She shook her head. "I think it's only a matter of time before they get close enough to harm us."

"That's a scary thought." Avery frowned. "I hope it's not true."

"I hope it's not too. But Avery, think about it. What would your brother do if he saw a human swimming toward him?" She looked up at her friend.

"Bernard?" She shuddered. "He would probably try to hurt him."

"Exactly. Now, what do you think a human would do if he saw a mermaid swimming toward him?" Kira raised an eyebrow.

"The same." Avery's eyes widened. "Because he would be scared."

"Yes. To him, we would be the same monster that he is to us. That's why we have to be prepared. Maybe humans aren't terrible creatures, but we don't know that for sure and they don't know that about us either." Kira swam toward the seaweed that covered the entrance to the room. "I need a break from all this. Carlos is waiting for me to play a game of toss the shell with him. Do you want to play with us?"

"Yes, I'd love to." Avery swam after her. "It would be a good idea to get our minds off of this."

"There he is!" Kira pointed to the lobster, who was scurrying up just outside of Coral Palace. "Carlos! Did you find a good shell?"

"I found two." He smiled as he held up a shell in each claw. "That should make the game even more challenging."

"I'm up for it!" Kira stretched her arms through the water. "I need to work off some stress!"

"Perfect!" Carlos tossed the shells into the water above his head. "Let the game begin!"

Kira lunged for the first shell she saw. As she swam toward it, she was rocked by Avery blasting past her.

"Mine!" Avery laughed as she snatched the shell.

Kira dove down to grab the other shell. When she reached for it, Carlos snatched it up just before she could get it.

"Not so fast, Kira!" He chuckled.

"No fair!" Kira swiped at the shell in his claw.

"Don't worry, I'll toss it again." He grinned. He tossed it high into the water. Instead of its beginning to sink down, the shell began to swirl upward.

"Oh no, I think a current has it! I'll get it!" Kira swam as fast as she could toward the shell. As she stretched out her hand to grasp it, she was blinded by a strange and bright light.

"What is that?" She shielded her eyes, but she still couldn't see past the glare.

CHAPTER 2

"Kira!" Avery swam up beside her. "Where is that light coming from?"

"I'm not sure." Kira sank down through the water. "I've never seen anything so bright in the water before."

"It glows much brighter than Bea." Avery stayed close to Kira. "Should we get closer? Maybe we will be able to see what it is?"

"I don't think we should." Kira took her hand. "If it's nothing we've seen before, it's possible that it's something human made."

"Do you think so?" Avery tightened her hand around Kira's.

"I'm not sure. But we shouldn't chance getting too close." She tugged Avery away from the bright light.

Once she swam away from it, her vision began to clear. She watched as a figure in black with two strange cylinders on its back swam past. The light shined from its head and moved when it turned.

As the light traveled toward them, Kira swam faster. She still clung to Avery's hand.

"Don't let it see us! Faster, Avery!"

"We have to get back to the palace!" Avery pointed to Carlos. "If we get to Carlos, we'll make it."

"No!" Kira tugged her in the other direction. "I'm sorry, Avery, I know you're scared, but we have to get as far away from the palace as we can."

"What?! Why?" Avery pulled back. "We might get caught!"

"It's better if we get caught than if all of Eldoris is discovered!" Kira gave her a firm tug and swam forward. "Hurry! If we can get to those rocks, we won't be seen!" She pointed to a large rock formation not far from them.

Avery began to swim with Kira instead of against her.

Kira's heart pounded. She could tell that the water around them was getting brighter and that meant the light had turned in their direction. Could it see them? She swam as fast as she could.

When she reached the rocks, she pulled Avery down beside her, then she peered around the edge of the rock.

"Do you think it saw us?" Avery whispered.

"I don't know." Kira peered out at the water beyond the rocks. The dark figure continued to swim. "But it can't be a human."

"It must be! You saw the tools it had." Avery tipped her head to the side. "What else could it be?"

"I don't know. But that creature has been under the water this whole time. Humans can't breathe under water. Right?"

"Well, we don't know that for sure." Avery peered around the edge of the rock as well. "Those are definitely human tools."

"Shh." Kira pulled her back behind the rocks. "It's coming this way."

"We can't stay here," Avery whispered. "There's nowhere to hide!"

"You're right. As soon as it gets around the edge of the rocks we'll be caught."

Kira's mind raced. She could only imagine what the creature would do to them. Whether or not it was a human, it was clearly on the hunt.

"We have to come up with a plan." She swished her tail through the water. As she did, a few bubbles rose up. Her eyes widened at the sight. "I've got it!" She swam close to Avery. "When the creature gets close, we both need to swish our tails as much as we can—just to make a lot of bubbles. Once we do that, the creature won't be able to see us. Then we'll swim away quickly." She held her hand out to Avery. "We have to stay together so we won't get lost."

"Are you sure it will work?" Avery shivered. "What if it can see through the bubbles?"

"It's my best idea. Can you think of anything better?"

"No." Avery frowned.

"Good, then when I say go, slap that tail as hard as you can, okay?" She met Avery's eyes.

"Yes, I'll do it." Avery nodded.

Kira swam to the edge of the rock again. She peered around it. Bright light swept through the water. It nearly blinded her. She winced, then squinted her eyes. Through the light, she could see the dark figure as it got closer. As her heart raced her tail twitched with the urge to start slapping. But she needed to wait for the right moment.

"When I say go, turn around and slap!" She looked over at Avery. "Got it?"

"Got it!" Avery nodded, her eyes wide.

When Kira looked back at the creature, the light briefly sent her into a daze. She blinked, then shouted.

"Go!" She flipped her body around and aimed her tail at the creature. She felt the water roll beside her as Avery did the same thing. As soon as Kira's tail pointed in the right direction, she began slapping it fiercely through the water.

Avery slapped her tail hard too. She gripped Kira's hand tightly.

The choppy water rocked Kira back and forth. A quick glance over her shoulder revealed that hundreds of bubbles were shooting up from her flailing tail.

"Now swim, Avery! Swim as fast as you can! But don't let go of my hand!" Kira swam forward as fast as she could. With her tail already tired from slapping so hard, she couldn't swim as fast as usual.

Avery struggled to keep up, but she kept her hand tightly wrapped around Kira's.

After she swam for some time, Kira dared to glance back over her shoulder. In the distance, she could still see the light. As she watched, it didn't seem to be getting any closer.

"I think we got away." Kira smiled.

"That's great." Avery gulped. "But do you have any idea where *away* is?"

Kira drank in the sight of the unfamiliar sea around them. It was full of rocks, coral, and strange skinny fish that she couldn't identify. When she looked up, she saw shards of sunlight pouring down through the water.

CHAPTER 3

"We're close to the surface." Kira narrowed her eyes as she stared up at the sunlight. "The sunlight shows that."

"How did we get so close?" Avery frowned. "We're not supposed to be anywhere near it."

"I guess that we swam fast and upward." Kira looked back in the direction of the light. Was it getting closer? "We should keep moving just in case."

"But which way?" Avery turned around in a slow circle. "None of this looks familiar."

"I'm not sure." Kira's heart dropped. Yes, they had evaded the creature, but what did that matter if they couldn't find their way home? She'd never been out in the open sea without someone to guide her. Not only that, but she had Avery to worry about too. "We'll figure it out, Avery. Let's just get a little further away from that light. That way." She pointed in the direction opposite that of the light. "I'm sure we can get to deeper water that way."

"Great." Avery smiled, but her voice trembled.

Kira swam forward and did her best to look confident. She sensed that Avery was very afraid. She didn't blame her. She was pretty scared herself. If only she hadn't decided to play toss the shell, maybe they wouldn't be in this mess.

She thought about how worried Carlos had to be. Had he told the others they'd gone missing? Maybe they would come looking for them. The thought both excited and worried her. If they came looking, they might just run into the creature with the light along the way.

"Kira?" Avery cleared her throat. "Don't you think the water is getting a little shallow?" Avery slowed down as a high shelf of rock came into view ahead of them.

"You're right." Kira had been so lost in thought that she hadn't noticed that there was only a few feet of water between them and the surface.

She thought about Trina putting her fingers through the surface of the water on their last adventure. Kira hadn't been interested in trying, but now with the sunlight so bright just above her, she felt a faint desire to explore it.

"Maybe once we get past the rock, the water will get deep again." Kira swam forward. "I'll go first."

As she swam over the rock, she felt the heat of the sun on her back. Was she so close that she could be seen by someone looking down at the water? The thought made her skin prickle with fear. She hoped it wasn't the case.

She swam faster, hoping to get to the deep water again.

Instead, to her horror, her fingertips glided through sand. Her stomach scraped across it.

"Kira, are you okay? Did you find deeper water?" Avery called out to her. "Kira, I'm pretty sure that light is getting closer behind us."

Kira's stomach twisted with fear. How was it possible that the water could be so shallow? She had never seen anything like it before. When she looked up, there were only a few inches of water above her—maybe a foot. If she lifted her head, she might even break the surface.

Terrified, she began to inch backwards.

"Don't come any closer, Avery. The water isn't getting deeper. It only gets more shallow." She eased herself back along the rocky shelf.

"Kira, we can't stay here," Avery whispered. "Look." She pointed back over her shoulder.

The light was much brighter. The creature swam closer.

"Shh, Avery." Kira's heart pounded.

"What are we going to do?" Avery whispered back.

"We have to go forward." Kira's mind spun at the thought. "It's our only choice. We have to swim forward, but we have to be very careful. The water is so shallow that our tails would break the surface. We'll have to pull ourselves along the sand. Like we did when we were babies, do you remember?"

"Before we could swim on our own?" Avery's eyes widened. "Are you serious?"

"I'm serious, Avery. If you swish your tail, you're going to send up a splash that anyone nearby will be able to see. Do you think you can do it? Can you crawl across the sand?" Kira looked into her friend's eyes.

"What choice do I have?" Avery frowned. "It's that or go back toward the light."

"I'll go first." Kira did her best to sound brave. "I'm sure we will find deeper water in no time."

"You keep saying that," Avery hissed. "But I'm starting to think you're wrong."

"Just trust me." Kira forced a smile to her lips. "We're on an adventure, right? No one we know has ever been in water this shallow."

"That's true." Avery looked up through the water. "Do you think we're near land? Is that why the water is so shallow?"

"It's possible." Kira tried not to panic.

"That means we might be near humans." Avery smiled. "Wouldn't it be amazing if we saw one?"

"No!" Kira huffed. "Listen to me, Avery, you have to stay focused. The goal here is not to get caught. Right? Not by that weird light-wielding creature and not by humans or other predators. Don't get distracted."

"You're right." Avery nodded. "I'll do my best."

"I'm going first. Just take it very slow. Remember to keep your head down and your tail still. Got it?" She stared at Avery.

"Got it." Avery smiled.

Kira didn't think she had it at all. In fact, she guessed that Avery might be daydreaming about what it would be like to spot a human.

She ignored her frustration and turned her attention upon moving forward. As she slid across the rock she wondered if she'd made the wrong decision by fleeing from the light in the first place. Even if they got to deeper water, would they ever be able to find their way home again?

CHAPTER 4

Kira continued along the sand. She dug her fingers into it and pulled her body forward. With her mind focused on getting to deeper water, she didn't notice what was beneath her at first. But when her fingertips hit something hard and smooth it drew her attention.

Beneath her was an assortment of shells. They varied in color and size so much that the sight of them made her heartbeat quicken. She'd never seen so much beauty in one place before. She scooped a few up in her hand as she continued forward.

She didn't dare to look back at Avery, as she might lift her head too far. The warm water sloshed over her skin. It felt wonderful.

For a moment she imagined what it would be like to feel the actual sun on her skin. Would it be even warmer?

She again felt a faint desire to break the surface. There was so much to discover—so much to explore.

Kira felt Avery's fingertips tickling her along the edge of her tail, the light touch reminding her to continue moving forward. But she couldn't resist snapping her fingers. The shells in her hand disappeared. She knew she would get a chance to look at them more closely later.

As she continued to inch forward, she looked for any sign of the water getting deeper. When she tipped her head to the right, she saw that the sand tilted downward. She began to shift her body in that direction.

A light touch on her tail let her know that Avery had shifted in that direction too.

As the sand tilted further, she began to swim downward. She willed her tail to keep still. She had to fight the urge to swish it through the water.

Once she was far enough down, she looked back over her shoulder at Avery.

Avery swam down to join her. "That was so weird." Avery whispered. "Did you see those amazing shells?"

"I did." Kira smiled. Then she watched the water for any sign of the light they had first seen.

As several seconds passed, she began to believe that they had finally evaded it.

"What do you think this place is?" Avery swam closer to the shallow water again. "How could it have so many beautiful shells?"

"Where the water meets the land, things wash up." Kira shivered. "Just like we almost did."

"Then you really do think we're near land?"

"Yes, I do." She swam over to Avery. "I also think we need to get back home as soon as we can."

"I agree." Avery stretched her arms out in front of her. "But I'm so tired. Do you think we can rest at least for a little while? Maybe I could collect some of those shells?"

"We can't risk going back into water that shallow." Kira pointed to a pile of seaweed on the sand below. "But that looks like a good place to rest. Doesn't it?"

"Yes, it does." Avery swam over to it and sprawled out across it. "Are you going to rest with me?"

"Yes." Kira swam toward her. Only then did she realize just how sore and tired her body was. Her tail hung limply as she crawled onto the seaweed. After being so afraid and swimming so fast, she had worn herself out completely. Still, she didn't think they were safe enough for her to sleep.

She gazed up through the water instead.

As she watched, the sunlight sparkled on the surface. She could make out movement, but not what was causing it. It seemed to glide through the air the way a fish might glide through the water.

As scared as she was of humans, she had to admit that she was curious too. She wondered what creatures might live on land. She wondered if they felt the same curiosity about what might live in the sea. Could humans really be so different when they looked so similar?

She thought about the weapons in the hidden room of the palace. It sure seemed like they had to belong to monsters. But maybe there was another purpose for them.

Not every mermaid was the same. Maybe not every human was the same either.

As Kira pondered these things, she didn't even notice when she drifted off to sleep. It wasn't until she felt the water ripple over her skin that she began to stir.

She became aware that she had been asleep and it must have been for quite some time, as the sunlight no longer sparkled in the water. With her heart in her throat she wondered what had caused the water to ripple.

She lifted her head enough to peer through the water, and when she did, she saw several figures swimming in her direction. They were too far away for her to decipher exactly who they were, but they would be on top of her and Avery in mere seconds.

Once more, they were trapped between unknown danger and the shallow water that they'd just crawled across.

"Avery." She shook the other mermaid awake, then put her finger to her lips. "Don't make a sound. We're not alone."

Avery's eyes widened as she looked in the direction of the figures.

Kira peered through the now-dark water. Were they humans? Were they sharks? She wasn't sure, but she knew one thing. They sure seemed to be in danger.

CHAPTER 5

"I think they see us," Avery whispered and huddled closer to Kira. "What are we going to do?"

"Just be still." Kira frowned.

There wasn't much else they could do. Going back into the shallow water would put them in danger and they wouldn't be able to move through it fast enough to escape. She could only hope that for some reason the figures would swim right past.

"Kira!" A voice called out to her from the group that swam toward them.

"Michelle?" Kira's heart skipped a beat. "Michelle, is that you?"

"Yes, it's us." Michelle swam closer. "Carlos came to find us when you swam away from him. He saw the light and he knew you needed help. By the time we came back you'd already swum off, but we were able to follow the creature with the light. We thought that we'd lost track of you."

"Are you two okay?" Trina looked at Kira and Avery. "Bernard was beside himself, but we told him we'd find you, Avery."

"We're okay." Avery smiled, then pressed her hand against

her chest. "You did give us quite a scare, though."

"Sorry about that," Trina whispered. "We didn't want to draw too much attention. Bethany has been so good at listening for possible predators, but we didn't want to take any chances."

"Bethany?" Kira's eyes widened as the mermaid inched forward. "You came to find us?"

"I was with Trina and Michelle in the throne room when Carlos came to find them. I thought maybe I could help." She tugged at her hair. "I can hear things in the water—a little better than other mermaids, I guess."

"I'm so glad that you're here." Kira smiled at her. Bethany was one of the shyest mermaids she'd ever known. "I'm so glad that you've all come to help us. I managed to get us lost, and to be honest, I wasn't sure how we were going to get back."

"Don't worry. I have these." Michelle lifted the gem necklace that hung around her neck. "They will show us the way home."

"Great!" Kira grinned.

"But there's no rush, is there?" Avery looked back toward the shallow water. "Kira and I are pretty sure that we are very close to land. Which means there may be a lot of humans around."

"All the more reason to get home quickly." Michelle crossed her arms.

"Hello? Did you forget about me?" Carlos ran up to the group. "Oh, Kira, I'm so happy to see you!" He scuttled straight to her. "Would you believe that no one would give me a ride?" He grabbed onto her hair and settled onto her back.

"That's not true, Carlos, I offered." Trina raised an eyebrow.

"Share a shoulder with that sea slug?" Carlos turned away. "Never."

"Bea and Carlos had a bit of a fight," Trina whispered to Kira. "Something about who is better at shell toss."

"That game again?" Kira frowned. "It's causing all kinds of trouble." She reached up and patted the top of Carlos's head. "I'm so glad that you were looking out for us, Carlos. If you hadn't gone for help, we might still be lost. I know I'm ready to go home."

"Wait, what about the shells?" Avery swished her tail through the water. "We can't let them leave without showing them the shells, Kira. It wouldn't be fair. Would it?"

"What shells?" Trina swam closer. "You've got my interest."

"If we're near land, then there are probably many shells around." Bethany looked toward the shallow water. "Shells gather near beaches."

"Beaches?" Kira looked at her. "What are those?"

"Strips of sand between land and sea." She smiled. "My mother has told me many things about the sea and land."

"She has? How does she know?" Kira tried to imagine what a beach might look like.

"She likes to study things. She's explored quite a bit." Bethany frowned as she looked down at the sand beneath her. "Please don't get her into trouble with the queen. I know it's against the rules, but this was when she was younger. She tells me about it because she thinks it will keep me from exploring too much—but all it really does is make me have so many more questions." She glanced among the other mermaids. "I would love to see the shells. I mean, if that's okay with everyone."

"Me too!" Trina grinned. "I can't wait to check them out."

"I don't know." Michelle put her hands on her hips. "It's risky if we are near land."

"It won't take long. Kira and I know right where they are. Don't we, Kira?" Avery smiled.

"Here." Kira snapped her fingers, then opened her hand. "These are some I collected."

"Oh wow!" Trina's eyes widened. "Look at the colors!

They're so beautiful!"

"There are more of these?" Michelle looked up at Kira curiously.

"Lots more." Kira nodded, then pointed to the shallow water. "Just over there. But we have to crawl on our stomachs. We can't even swish our tails. The water is so low that if we lift our heads, we'll break the surface."

"Break the surface?" Trina got a whimsical look on her face. "I'd love to try that again."

"Absolutely not." Michelle pointed a finger straight at her. "You will not break the surface. No one will. Understand?" Michelle reached up and adjusted the crown on her head. "As a princess of Eldoris, I command that no one is to break the surface."

"We won't, we promise." Avery clasped her hands together. "We should go soon—before the sunlight comes through the water again."

"Fine. We'll each collect a few shells. Then we'll head back home." Michelle looked at Kira. "Would you like to show us where to go?"

"I will." Kira swam toward the shallow water. "Go slow and keep low." As she crawled through the sand, she felt the shells beneath her. "It's hard to see them with no sunlight."

"I can help with that." Bea crawled forward and began to glow. As her light illuminated the shells, the others all marveled over their beauty.

Kira noticed that Avery didn't seem that interested in shells. Instead, she swam toward the water that was even more shallow.

"Avery? You're getting too shallow. You should come back." Kira swam toward her.

"I just want to see, just for a second." She looked back at Kira. "It can't be that bad, can it? It's night, it's quiet. I just want one quick peek."

CHAPTER 6

"Avery, no!" Kira grabbed for her tail. "Don't you dare break the surface."

"Stop!" Avery tried to free her tail. "I just want one quick look. It can't do any harm!" As she thrashed to get free from Kira's grasp, she sent ripples through the water.

Kira tried to hold on tighter, but the tighter she held, the more Avery thrashed.

She thought about the desire that she'd felt to break the surface. Was it possible that breaking the surface had its own subtle pull, not unlike a current or a strong wave?

She felt Avery slip free and her own body lurched ahead.

As Kira tried to get herself straightened out, she lifted her head. All at once she felt water drip from her hair, her cheeks, and her chin. She opened her mouth and it filled with a strange sensation that tickled the inside of her throat. All above her were strange lights in a sea of darkness.

It took her a few seconds to realize what had happened. She had broken the surface of the water with her entire head. Even her shoulders had emerged from the water.

It was horrifying for her. Even worse, she couldn't breathe.

The more her mouth and nose filled with the strange dry air that surrounded her, the more she felt as if she might suffocate.

She felt hands on her tail and waist. As she was pulled back down under the water, she caught a glimpse of a long wooden structure along with several boats. She also saw a sea of white sand that stretched right up a small hill. Then her head plunged back under the water and she could breathe again.

"Kira, are you okay?" Avery clung to her. "I'm so sorry, I didn't mean to do that to you. Honestly I didn't!"

"Avery, she could have been killed!" Michelle shouted. "You are in big trouble!"

"Wait, no." Kira cleared her throat, which still felt funny. "It's not her fault. There is a draw. When you get into shallow enough water, you feel it. It's as if the land is calling to you." She looked at the others. "Did you feel it?"

"Yes!" Trina's eyes widened. "I did. I thought I was going crazy."

"Me too." Bethany admitted softly. "But I thought it was because I really did want to break the surface." She looked at Kira. "What was it like? What did you see?"

Kira thought about the structure, the boats, and the strange sea above it all. She knew that her friends wanted to know every detail, but she felt strange sharing it. What if it drove Avery or Bethany to break the surface?

"I saw some things." She clutched her hands together. "I think if everyone has their shells now, we should head back home." She rubbed her hand along her throat. "I couldn't breathe above the water. It wore me out to try."

"Yes, I think that would be best." Michelle looked sternly at Avery. "And you need to stay right next to me. I don't want any more mishaps."

"I'm so sorry." Avery looked down at her hands. "I really didn't mean to. I just—I had to know. We were so close and maybe we'll never be this close again. All Bernard ever talks about is how dangerous humans are—how terrible the human world is." She looked up with tears in her eyes. "But I just don't believe it. I don't believe that it could be so terrible. I've seen the beautiful things they create. I'm so very curious about all that. Why is it fair that our king and queen have set these rules about what we can and can't do? Shouldn't we be able to choose for ourselves what we want to explore and learn about?"

"Don't talk like that." Michelle crossed her arms. "My mother and father made these rules to keep us all safe. They do it because they know what dangers are out there and they want to protect us. It's not a bad thing."

"No, maybe it's not a bad thing." Trina whispered. "But it isn't really fair either, is it? For us to just have to wonder? I know all the stories we've heard about humans have been bad. But what if there's more to them than we know? What if they are as different as all of us? What if there are things they can teach us? Maybe we could learn to make some of the things they've created."

"We don't need any of it." Kira put her hands on her hips. "Nothing they've made is more important than our safety. Especially not all those weapons."

"Kira, you know that we're curious. Please, won't you tell us what you saw?" Bethany stared at her. "Maybe if you do, we'll all feel better about going back home instead of getting a chance to explore."

"I saw a long wooden structure and some boats." Her heart skipped a beat as she recalled it. "Which means lots of humans are probably around. I also saw a sea of white sand." She brushed her hand across her throat again. "It must be the beach that you talked about, Avery."

"And?" Avery swam closer. "Was there anything else? Did you see anything else?"

"I saw perhaps the most stunning thing I've ever seen." Kira remembered the beauty of the sea above her head. "There was an ocean of darkness as wide as the sea we swim in. It was spotted with all these little lights, like there were thousands of sea slugs floating out there." She smiled. "It's something I will never forget." She shivered. "But it's also something that I never want to see again."

CHAPTER 7

"Why not?" Avery swam closer to Kira. "How could you not want to see something like that again?"

"I don't know. Maybe it was because I couldn't breathe!" Kira rolled her eyes. "It's terrifying up there!"

"If you say so." Avery frowned as she sank down into the sand. "I guess I'll never know."

"Me either." Bethany crossed her arms. "And we're so close. There's land up there! I want to see it so badly. Could it really hurt for us all to have a look?"

"It's out of the question." Michelle swept her hands through the water in front of her. "We've already taken too many risks. Besides, not everyone wants to do it."

"I wouldn't mind." Trina suddenly spoke up. "I'd love to see what's out there. I mean, it's best to know what we're up against, right? None of us really know for sure. We couldn't even figure out if that figure with the light was human or not. So, if they do come for us, we won't even recognize them!"

"That's a good point, Trina." Michelle narrowed her eyes.

"Don't forget that we can't breathe up there!" Kira put her hands on her hips.

"True, but once you were back in the water you were okay." Bethany met Kira's eyes. "I know you found it frightening, but the way you describe the dark sea with lights in it, it just makes me want to see it."

"Okay, here's my decision." Michelle swam closer to the other mermaids. "Anyone who wants to break the surface can do so, just this once." She looked at each of them in turn. "But it has to be our secret. If my mother and father find out about this, they will not be pleased."

"I won't tell." Avery smiled.

"Neither will I." Bethany rubbed her hands together.

"Kira?" Trina looked straight at her. "What about you?"

Kira frowned. She didn't want to deny her friends the excitement of breaking the surface, but she also worried that it might make them think it would be okay to do it all the time.

"I broke the surface by accident. It's still a very dangerous thing to do." She threw her hands up. "But if it's what you want, I will keep your secret."

"That is very kind of you, Kira." Carlos scuttled over to her. "I will stay with you while the others break the surface."

"Thank you, Carlos."

"It's now or never." Michelle looked over at the other three mermaids. "Remember, we are only going to be up there for a short time. Break the surface, look around, then duck right back under the water. Got it?"

"Got it," Avery squeaked. "I can't wait!"

"Are we all going to do it together?" Trina smiled. "I think that would be the most fun."

"Let's do it." Michelle nodded. She led the way toward the more shallow water.

Kira followed after them, with Carlos on her shoulder. When the others went forward even farther, she hung back. A desire stirred in her to break the surface again, but she ignored it. She'd had her taste of the other world and she much preferred the safety of the sea.

She watched as her friends held hands, then broke through the surface together. Her heart pounded for the few seconds they were above the water. It continued to race as they sank back down below the surface.

All but one.

Avery remained above the surface.

"Wow!" Michelle spun around under the water. "That was stunning."

"Avery!" Kira pointed toward the water. "She's still up there and she's swimming forward."

"Grab her!" Michelle called out.

All of the mermaids wrapped their arms around Avery's tail and tugged her back down through the water. Avery struggled a little. As she did, Kira slammed into something hard. It felt like a rock. She twisted around in an attempt to see what it was.

Avery thrashed as she began to breathe again under the water. Her body trembled. Kira let go of her tail, her arm still sore from whatever she had slammed into.

"Avery, are you okay?" She looked into her friend's eyes, which stared upward.

"It was so pretty." Avery reached her hand up through the water toward the surface. "Did you all see it? The lights in the black sea?"

"It's sky." Bethany whispered as she hovered close to Avery. "My mother has told me about it. It stretches above the land and sea everywhere. It's sky."

"Sky?" Avery sat up in the sand. "What does it do? What is it for?"

"I'm not sure." Bethany clasped her hands together. "But you're right, it is very pretty."

"Sky." Michelle repeated. "Even its name sounds beautiful."

"I've never seen anything like it." Trina closed her eyes. "I never want to forget it."

"Avery, why did you stay up there so long?" Kira looked at her.

"I don't know exactly." Avery frowned. "I didn't do it on purpose. I just got caught up in the sky and the way the air around me felt. It was like it touched my skin. Did anyone else feel that?"

"Yes, I did." Bethany smiled. "It was strange but wonderful."

"I thought it was a little creepy," Michelle whispered.

"It tickled." Trina laughed.

"Yes! That's it!" Michelle laughed as well.

While the others discussed their adventure, Kira turned her attention back to her sore arm.

"Oh, Kira, what happened?" Trina looked at her. "Your arm is bleeding."

"It is?" Kira twisted her arm to get a better look. A long jagged scratch ran across the back of her arm. A bit of blood spilled out of it. "It's not too bad." She frowned. "I bumped into something. I'm not sure what it was. Bea, do you think you could light up the water over here?"

"Sure." Bea crawled off of Trina's arm and toward Kira. As she did, she began to glow. The water lit up around Kira.

Right away she spotted a large square-shaped object. It appeared to be made out of metal and had bars that lined each of its sides.

"What is that?" Bethany swam forward.

"Don't get too close." Michelle frowned. "We have no idea what it could be used for."

"There's something inside." Kira narrowed her eyes. "There's something moving inside of it."

CHAPTER 8

"Creepy!" Bea crawled right back to Trina's arm and climbed on. Her glow was still bright enough to reveal the strange object.

"It must be some kind of trap." Avery inched closer. "I've seen something similar at the Coral Palace. It has these." She touched one of the bars.

Suddenly the trap came alive with movement and clacking. It shook.

"What's inside of it?" Trina edged her way closer.

"I'm not sure, but there are so many." Kira grabbed two of the bars and pulled herself closer. As she looked into the eyes of one of the creatures, her heart skipped a beat. "Lobsters!"

"What?" Carlos poked his head over her shoulder and looked inside the cage. "She's right! It's full of lobsters!"

"Set us free." One of the lobsters stuck his claws through the cage. "Please, set us free."

"Of course we will." Carlos looked over at the others. "Won't we?"

"Yes." Michelle grabbed the door of the cage and tugged at it. "It's stuck."

"It's held closed by this." Bethany lifted up a thick metal lock. She tugged hard on it. "It won't come open."

"It's a trap." Carlos swam backwards a short distance. "I've heard of these things. Lobsters go in and never come out again."

"Please." Another lobster came up to the bars of the cage. "We'll never be able to escape without your help."

"We'll figure out a way." Trina narrowed her eyes. "We're going to get you out of there."

"We're going to need a tool." Avery swam forward. "Something that can break the lock or the bars."

"A rock?" Kira glanced around the area for any loose rocks. "I don't see too many."

"The ones I see are too small." Trina plucked a rock no bigger than a pebble from the sand. "It's not going to help us."

"If only Bernard were here with that tool the humans made." Avery crossed her arms. "I'm sure that would help."

"This also appears to be a tool that the humans made. Keep that in mind." Michelle pointed to the trap. "It's strong and it's made out of unbreakable material. We're going to have a tough time getting it open. Maybe we should just bring it back to Eldoris with us. I'm sure my mother and father can come up with a way to get the lobsters free."

"Can we swim with it?" Kira grabbed one of the bars and tried to lift it. "It's not too heavy." She smiled. "I think we could get it home."

"Great, let's all take a side." Avery grabbed one side of the trap. Bethany took the next side. Trina grabbed the last side.

"I'll use the necklace to lead us home." Michelle peered into the trap at the lobsters. "Don't worry, we'll have you home before you know it."

"It won't work." One of the lobsters hung her head. "You can't move the trap."

"Sure we can, it's not too heavy." Kira smiled as she pulled the trap forward. It moved easily—until it didn't. She tugged harder. It wouldn't budge. "What's it stuck on?" She frowned.

"A chain." Carlos swam behind the trap. "There's a chain that connects to the back of it."

"A chain?" Michelle frowned. "Where does it go?"

"Toward the beach." Carlos stuck his claw inside the trap. "Don't worry, we're going to get you out."

"You can't," another lobster sighed. "It's hopeless."

"It's not." Kira touched the claw of one of the lobsters. "We'll find a way."

"I remember seeing long metal poles on the wooden structure," Bethany piped up. "They looked like tools of some kind. Maybe something like that would help?"

"We might be able to pry the trap open with something like that." Trina nodded.

"But it's outside of the water." Kira looked up toward the surface. It was still dark, but it seemed a little less dark. "I don't think the night will last much longer."

"Then we're going to have to move quickly." Michelle grabbed the bars on the trap again. "The trap is strong, but I think with a tool we could get them free."

"That seems impossible." Kira shook her head.

"What choice do we have, Kira?" Michelle met her eyes. "We can't just leave them here, can we? I may be princess of Eldoris, but that doesn't mean it's not my duty to protect all sea creatures."

"Please don't leave them here." Carlos clung to the bars of the trap. "They deserve to be free."

"Yes, I'm sure they do." Kira frowned.

"Let's start by following the chain." Trina swam forward. "If we can get that loose, then we can carry the trap back to Eldoris with us."

"I'll swim with you." Avery started forward.

"We'll all go." Michelle glanced around at the others. "We might need all of our combined strength to get the chain free. Carlos, you stay here and keep an eye on the lobsters, okay?"

"I will." Carlos saluted her with one claw.

"And Bea, would you mind lighting the way for us?" Michelle looked at the sea slug. "I know you must be tired from glowing so much, but if we want to free the chain, we'll need to see what we're doing."

"I don't mind. I can glow all night." She wiggled her small body, then surged forward on the sand. "Follow me!"

Her glow revealed the chain that ran along the sand. It wasn't as thick as the bars on the trap, but it was too strong for them to snap.

Kira followed the others forward, aware that the further they swam, the more shallow the water would get. She wanted to save the lobsters, but was it even possible?

CHAPTER 9

"Look!" Michelle pointed ahead of them. "The chain runs up out of the water."

"There are wooden poles over here." Avery swam toward them. "Several of them."

"They must be holding up that wooden structure we saw." Bethany narrowed her eyes. "They are supports to hold it up."

"That makes sense." Michelle nodded. "So, the trap is in the sea and the chain runs up to that wooden structure. Is it so that humans can pull the trap out of the water?"

Trina shuddered at the thought. "They created a tool to trap lobsters and pull them out of the sea."

"That means they could create the same kind of trap for us." Kira's stomach flipped at the thought. "It also means that we're not going to be able to break the chain."

"Let me take a look." Avery swam toward the surface. "I'm sure there's something that can help us."

"Wait, Avery." Michelle shook her head. "We have to be very careful now. We're very close to the wooden structure, where humans might be. What if one of them sees us?"

"What choice do we have?" Avery shook her head. "There

has to be something up there that we can use to help the lobsters."

"I will take a look." Bea slid toward one of the wooden poles. "I can climb up and see what's up there."

"Bea, will you be okay outside of the water?" Kira frowned.

"For a short time." Bea nodded. "I won't be long."

"I'm not sure that's such a good idea." Michelle crossed her arms.

"Let her go." Kira touched Michelle's arm. "She wants to help. I'll keep a close eye on her."

Kira swam over to the wooden pole that Bea began to climb. It took some time for the slug to break the surface of the water and then scale the length of the pole. Once she did, Kira saw her stick her head out to look around.

Kira did her best to watch her from under the water. Her heart pounded as she wondered if her friend would be safe. When Bea finally began to climb back down, she felt some relief.

Bea slid back under the water and crawled over to Kira's arm for a rest.

"Did you see anything we could use?" Bethany swam over to her.

"I saw something interesting." Bea tipped her head back toward the trap. "Remember the lock on the front?"

"Yes, I've seen something like it before at the Coral Palace." Avery nodded. "It has a special hole that something must fit into in order to open it."

"Yes, it does. I think maybe I found that something. It's hanging off the edge of the wooden structure, right near where the chain runs up onto it. I can't be sure that it's the right something, but it looks like it might be the right shape." She crawled off of Kira's arm and onto Trina's shoulder. "I'm not sure that it will work, but it might be worth a try."

"It would be easier than trying to break the lock or pry the trap open." Michelle nodded. "But how will we get it?"

"We'd have to break the surface again." Avery frowned.

"Even if we did break the surface, none of us would be able to reach it." Trina looked up through the surface of the water. "The wooden structure is too high for us."

"Maybe one of us could jump?" Avery suggested.

"No." Michelle shook her head. "That is far too dangerous. The splash would draw too much attention."

"I'll go get it. But I'll need Carlos's help." Kira smiled as a plan formed in her mind.

"It's too risky," Michelle protested.

"It's my risk to take." Kira looked at the others. "It's my fault we're here in the first place. I'll take the chance."

"Kira, you only swam off the way you did to protect Eldoris from being discovered." Avery hugged her.

"Maybe, but it still brought us here. Now I need to find a way to help these lobsters and get us home." Kira hugged her back.

"You don't have to do this. I'm the princess. It's my duty." Michelle swam forward.

"No, Michelle. That's exactly why you can't do it. You saw how hard it was for Avery to come back under the water. We can't take any chances that you wouldn't come back. I've already made my choice. I will be the one to go."

"I'll stay with you." Bethany met her eyes. "Just in case you run into any trouble."

"Thank you." Kira's heart began to pound. "First I need to see if Carlos will help."

She swam back toward the trap full of lobsters. When she reached it, Carlos was in the middle of a song.

"Don't worry...about a thing!" He spun around and waved his claws through the air. "Mermaids gonna make everything alright!" He shook his back end and flashed a smile in the direction of the lobsters.

A few of them laughed.

Kira did her best to hold in her own laughter. Seeing Carlos dance and sing brightened her attitude, but she still wondered if he was right. Would everything be alright?

"Kira, did you find a tool?" Carlos smiled at her.

"Actually, I think I did." She stared at him as a plan formed in her mind.

"Where is it?" He glanced around as the other mermaids approached.

"I'm looking at it." She crossed her arms. "If you're willing."

"Anything you ask I will do!" He clacked his claws. "Whatever it takes to set my friends free!"

"Great." She offered him her hair to climb up on. "You're going to have to climb a little higher for this to work."

"Higher?" He peeked over her shoulder.

"Higher." She nodded.

He climbed up along the back of her neck. "Is this better?"

"Higher." Kira patted the top of her head.

CHAPTER 10

"You want me to climb onto the top of your head?" Carlos peeked around the side of Kira's face to look at her. "Are you sure about that?"

"Yes. We're going to need those claws of yours to get the tool."

She began to swim back toward the wooden poles. As she did, she imagined her plan. With Carlos's help, she hoped that they'd be able to get the piece of metal that would fit into the lock. If it didn't work, maybe they could come up with something else. But it was worth a try.

As she reached the wooden pole, she looked up to the surface. Light sparkled through the water.

"Oh no!" She frowned. "The sun is rising."

"This is too dangerous now." Michelle swam up beside her. "We'll have to wait until it gets dark again."

"We can't!" Carlos cried out. "The humans might pull in the trap before then. We'll have no way to save my friends."

"I'm sorry, but it's too much of a risk." Michelle looked straight at Kira. "You could be seen, and if you are, we could put all of Eldoris in danger."

"I understand, Michelle." Kira looked into her friend's eyes. Her heart ached as she realized what she would have to do. "I'm sorry, but I don't have a choice."

She broke through the surface of the water and grabbed the wooden pole.

Michelle caught her tail with her hands and tugged.

Kira clung to the pole as Carlos wobbled back and forth on top of her head.

As Michelle pulled harder, Kira clung tighter. Finally, she felt Michelle let go of her tail, then she became aware of the thick air as it pushed against her skin. She felt the tickle in her throat. She knew that she wouldn't be able to stay out of the water for long.

She used her arms to pull herself up higher on the pole. Then she tipped her head in the direction of the metal piece that dangled from the side of the wooden structure.

"The key?" Carlos pointed at it, then leaned down over the top of Kira's head and peered into her eyes.

Kira nodded carefully. Without being able to breathe, she had no ability to speak.

Carlos got the message. He lunged toward the key with his claw outstretched. As he did, he slid on Kira's slick wet hair.

Just before he would have slipped off and crashed into the water, she reached up with one hand to steady him. He stretched his claw out and tried again.

"Got it!" he cried out, just before a quiet splash. "Uh, had it, then dropped it." He coughed.

As Kira peered up at the wooden structure, she heard something strange. Heavy thumps. The pole she clung to trembled a little.

"Morning, John!" a voice called out. "Should have a good haul today!"

The thumps got closer.

Kira's body trembled, not just from fear, but also from not breathing. She knew if she dropped down too quickly into the water she would create a splash.

She did her best to ease herself down carefully. As her head sank under the water, she saw a face peer over the edge of the wooden structure.

"What is that?" he called out. "There's something on this side of the pier! Something strange!"

"John, have you been watching those monster movies again?" another voice called out.

"No, it's not a monster. It's a—well, I don't know what it is. A lobster sitting on a human head?"

Kira swam down quickly. She worried that the man on the pier would jump in to search for her.

A second later, though, he let out a shout that made the water vibrate.

"Where's my key?!"

Kira could barely talk as she was finally able to breathe again.

"The key." She pointed to the sand. "It's somewhere down there."

All of the mermaids began to search, as did Carlos.

"Got it!" Carlos cried out as he held up his claw. "Not going to drop it this time."

"Let's go!" Avery took the key from him and swam as quickly as she could back toward the trap. As she swam, the trap began to slide back toward her. "Oh no! He's pulling it in!"

"Everyone grab on!" Michelle called out.

She grabbed the bars of the trap. The other mermaids joined in—all but Avery, who swam around to the front with the key.

Kira watched as Avery did her best to get the key into the lock.

"I can hear them." Bethany looked up through the water. "I

can hear them shouting. He is saying that his trap is stuck. He's asking other humans for help."

A hard tug yanked them all backwards through the water.

"One more tug like that and we'll all break the surface!" Trina clung to the trap. "Pull back hard, everyone!"

Kira, Trina, Bethany, and Michelle all pulled hard on the trap. As they did, Avery opened the lock. The door of the trap swung open in the same moment that they all heard a loud splash.

The lobsters scurried out of the cage just as two humans tumbled down through the water.

"Uh, I think we pulled too hard." Trina's eyes widened.

"Swim!" Michelle cried out. "As fast as you can!"

She led the way.

"Be free, my friends!" Carlos waved to the lobsters as he clung to Kira's hair.

The lobsters clambered over each other. They created a shield around the mermaids, blocking them from view.

The two humans swam upward, eager to get out of the water.

The mermaids continued to swim as fast as they could toward the deeper water.

"Are they following us?" Michelle looked back over her shoulder.

"No, I don't think so," Kira called back. She looked back once more. She saw lobsters racing after them, but no humans. "I think we're safe."

"Safe?" Michelle spun around to face her. "You think we're safe?"

"Michelle, I'm sorry." Kira frowned. "I had to set them free."

"And you were seen!" Michelle put her hands on her hips. "By a human!"

"I know." Kira winced. "But I don't think he knew what he

saw. He didn't see my tail. Just my head—and Carlos." She reached back and patted his claw. "He was so brave."

"Listen, everyone, we discovered something important today." Avery swam closer to Kira and Michelle.

"That Kira doesn't think she has to follow the rules?" Michelle raised an eyebrow.

"No, that we can understand humans." Avery looked at Kira. "You understood what they said. We all did."

"That's true." Kira narrowed her eyes. "I didn't even think about it, but I understood them."

"It's good to know that we share the same language." Avery wrapped her arms around Kira. "And it's even better to know that you were brave enough to save those lobsters, Kira."

"Michelle's right, I did break the rules." Kira frowned. "It's okay if you want to tell the king and queen, Michelle."

"No, Avery is right." Michelle hugged Kira as well. "You saved them, even when I was too scared to do it. You were very brave."

All of the other mermaids gathered close in a group hug.

"Now we know just how dangerous the humans are." Michelle swam forward. "They trap creatures like us. We need to get back to Eldoris and warn everyone."

Kira nodded.

She swam after the other mermaids, but she looked back once toward the wooden pole that held up the pier. Yes, the humans built traps, but they also built other amazing things. She recalled the friendly tone of the man's voice as he'd greeted his companion.

Did humans have friends just like mermaids did?

If so, could humans really be so bad?

BOOK 4: AVERY

CHAPTER 1

Avery swam out of her shell and stretched her arms above her head. Ever since she'd returned to Eldoris from the deep sea, she'd been sleepier than usual. Maybe it was from all the adventure or maybe it was from all the stress. Either way, she usually woke up later than the other mermaids.

She swam out into the water and found many of her friends were already hard at work. The mermaids had decided to create some protection around Coral Palace. They had been working hard to pile rocks and shells up to form a wall.

"Good morning." Avery swam over to Bethany. "How's it going so far?"

"Don't tell the others I said this, but not well." Bethany frowned. "Every time a strong current comes through, the shells and rocks topple over. Early this morning a whale happened by and we lost the entire front wall." She lowered her voice. "I don't think this is going to do anything to keep us safe."

"You might be right about that." Avery picked up a shell and added it to the pile. "But it's something to make us feel calmer, I guess. After seeing the lobsters in that trap, I guess we're all a little extra sensitive about things." She noticed Michelle swimming above them. "What is she up to?"

"I'm not sure. She's been swimming back and forth close to the surface all morning." Bethany looked up at Michelle too. "Maybe she just wants to get some sun."

"Maybe. I think I'll find out." Avery swam up toward Michelle. The closer she got to the surface, the warmer the water became. She smiled at the sensation and recalled what it had been like to actually break the surface. Feeling air on her skin for the first time had been both thrilling and shocking. She couldn't deny that she still had a strong urge to experience it again.

"Avery, it's about time you got up." Michelle smiled at her.

"I've been so sleepy lately." She shook her head. "I guess it's because of all the dreams I've been having."

"Dreams? You didn't tell me about any dreams." Michelle swam closer to her.

"It's nothing." Avery smiled. "What are you doing up here?"

"Keeping watch. Up here, I can see if a ship floats towards us or if there are any humans splashing into the water." She narrowed her eyes. "We can't be too careful—at least not until the wall is done."

"Yeah, about that..." Avery looked back down at her friends hard at work. "I'm not so sure it's the best plan."

"It's the only one we have right now." Michelle shivered despite the warm water. "I can't imagine what would happen if one of us got stuck in those cages. Not only would it be horrible for the mermaid, but the entire human world would soon learn all about us. We can't take that chance. We have to find a way to stay safe. This is the best we can do."

"I understand what you're saying, but wouldn't it make more sense to learn more about the humans? I mean, even if we can get the wall to stand, it will only protect us a little. Maybe if we learn more about the humans, we can prevent them from even getting near our world." Avery shrugged. "It's just an idea."

"It's a good idea." Michelle stretched out on her back and floated. "I can almost see past the surface when I do this."

"Really?" Avery stretched out beside her. "Oh wow!"

"It's dazzling, isn't it?" Michelle sighed. "Don't tell anyone else I said this, but it's hard for me not to break the surface."

"Me too!" Avery looked over at her. "It's like it's calling to me, inviting me to just poke my head out."

"Exactly." Michelle turned over and looked at her. "Which is why we have to be so careful. We don't know anything about this other world. It could be full of strange magic. It could lure us away from home and make us forget everything."

"It could." Avery bit into her bottom lip, then shook her head. "But even if it has strange magic, we still need to know. We have to figure out what we're dealing with. The more we learn, the better off we'll be."

"We've been studying all of the items from the human world that we've collected. What more do you think we can do?" Michelle met her eyes.

"Maybe we could explore a little more? Maybe we could take another journey?" Avery's heart pounded at the thought. "We learned so much last time. Now we know we can understand the humans when they speak."

"We also know that they set traps to capture sea creatures." Michelle crossed her arms. "We know just how dangerous the human world is and how risky it can be for us to be anywhere near it. It's safer for us to stay here."

"You're right, it may be safer to stay away from it." Avery stared at her. "But the human world isn't one place. It isn't just on land. The ships can travel anywhere, which means there really isn't a safe place for us to be. If we keep trying to find new places to hide, there might not be anywhere in the ocean left for us to go."

"I hadn't really thought about that." Michelle looked up at the surface of the water again. "You're right, they've already invented so much. They will always come up with new ways to explore the ocean. I'll talk to my parents about it and see what they think. I can't make any promises, though. After our last adventure, they have become very protective of all of us."

"I understand. Maybe they just need to realize how brave we are." Avery looked up at the surface. "I don't want to spend the rest of my life wondering what's really up there."

CHAPTER 2

As Avery swam back down toward the palace, she noticed Trina swimming up to her.

"Hi, Avery. What were you and Michelle talking about? It looked pretty serious."

"It was." Avery caught Trina's hand and tugged her away from the crowd of mermaids. "I asked her if we could try to learn more about the human world."

"You did?" Trina's eyes widened.

"You did?" A sea slug poked her head out from under Trina's hair and peered at Avery. "What did she say?"

"She's going to talk to the king and queen about it. But she didn't seem too optimistic. I just hope that they will consider it." She looked at Trina. "You agree with me, don't you? We need to find out more so that we can do everything we can to protect our world."

"I do agree, but I also know why the king and queen would be worried. We had a pretty close call last time and Michelle is their daughter. What if something had happened to her?" Trina frowned. "They have to make the best decision for all of us, not just for a few."

"That's true. I just think that the more we know, the safer we'll be. Maybe if we volunteer to be the ones to go explore, they'll be more likely to agree. Would you want to go with me?" She glanced over at the wall. "It seems like a better way to spend our time than this."

"I'd absolutely want to join you. If you think it would help, I would tell the queen that." She swam beside Avery. "What about Kira? She might want to come along."

"I haven't talked too much to her lately. She seems a little down, though." Avery frowned. "I planned to speak to her today to make sure that she's okay. I was thinking Bethany would like to come along too. She seems very interested in learning about the humans."

"Good idea." Trina nodded. "Let's go talk to Kira first. I think she's working in the seaweed garden." She swam toward the garden.

Avery swam a short distance behind her. She doubted that Kira would be interested in joining them. She'd already been frightened of the humans before they'd discovered the traps and Avery guessed that she was even more afraid now. Still, it was important to find out if she was okay.

Avery heard Trina call out as she swam through some tall seaweed just ahead of her. "Kira!"

"Ah!" Kira flipped backwards, startled by her friend. "Trina! Stop sneaking up on me!"

"I'm sorry!" Trina laughed. "You're just so cute when you do a back flip."

"It's not funny!" Kira crossed her arms. "Do it again and I'll send Carlos after you."

"Did someone say Carlos?" The lobster emerged from a pile of seaweed. He clacked his claws through the water.

"Settle down, Carlos." Bea, the sea slug, crept forward on Trina's shoulder. "We're just here to visit."

"Good." Carlos pointed his claw at her. "But if you give Kira any trouble, it'll be snip snip for you!" He snapped his claws.

"Eek!" Bea ducked back into Trina's hair.

"Stop it, you're scaring her." Trina frowned. "Listen, I know you're both frightened after what happened."

"Frightened?" Carlos scuttled toward her. "There were traps! Traps with lobsters in them! I am more than frightened."

"Me too." Kira shivered. "I can't even imagine what those humans are up to." She paused, then glanced down at her hands. "But..."

"But?" Avery swam closer to her. "But what?"

"I haven't been able to stop thinking about them either." She looked up at her friends. "They know so much, they've created so much. What if there are things they know that could help us?"

"I think it's possible." Avery nodded. "I think we need to find out more about them."

"We both do." Trina glanced at Avery. "We're hoping that the king and queen will agree and let us go exploring again."

"Really?" Kira looked between them. "You both want to go back?"

"Now that we've found land, it's hard not to want to learn more." Trina shrugged.

"And I think there is a lot more to humans than what we've seen. Like you said, maybe there are things we could learn from them." Avery looked at Kira. "We thought you might want to join us—if they say that we can go..."

"Me?" Kira smiled somewhat. "Really?"

"Yes, of course." Avery reached for her hand. "You were so brave. I know how scary it was for you, but we could really use you on our team."

"I have been thinking about it." Kira twirled some of her hair on her finger. "But you're right, it does still seem pretty scary. I guess if the queen says it's okay, I'd be willing to go. I certainly wouldn't want you two going without me."

"Great." Avery smiled. "That makes three of us."

"Don't forget about me!" Carlos swung his claw through the water.

"Or me!" Bea poked her head out again.

"That's right." Trina laughed. "That makes five of us."

"Hopefully Bethany will want to tag along too." Avery glanced around. "I haven't seen her yet this morning. Have either of you?"

"I saw her sneak off after breakfast." Kira raised an eyebrow. "It looked like she was up to something."

"Really?" Avery frowned. "Which way did she go?"

"Right back into the palace." Kira shrugged. "She's always curious about something."

"Yes, she is. We're headed that way to speak to the queen. Hopefully we'll find her first." Avery turned to swim toward the Coral Palace.

"I'll come with you." Kira swam after them.

"Wait for me!" Carlos grabbed onto Kira's hand and hitched a ride on her back.

"What could she be up to in the palace?" Trina frowned.

"I think I have a pretty good idea." Avery swam faster. "Hopefully she doesn't get caught!"

CHAPTER 3

As Avery suspected, she found Bethany in the secret room hidden far below the entrance of the Coral Palace. Here, the queen stored her collection of items that she believed belonged to humans. It was off limits to most, including Bethany. The queen had given permission to her daughter, Michelle, and to Trina and Kira to study the contents of the room. She had not given the same permission to Bethany.

"Bethany, what are you doing in here?" Avery put her hands on her hips. "You're not supposed to be here."

"Neither are you." Bethany smiled.

"She's with me." Trina crossed her arms. "Bethany, you could get into a lot of trouble if the queen caught you here."

"I know, I'm sorry." She swam up to them. "It's just that there's so much to discover. I just wanted a chance to look through everything. It might be years before I get to glimpse anything human again."

"It might not be as long as you think." Kira peered at a stack of strange rods that stood against the wall of the room. "What do you think these are for?"

"Careful!" Bethany swam close to her. "There are sharp bits on the end."

"Hooks." Avery nodded as she noticed the glint of metal in the water. "They're for fishing."

"Fishing?" Trina turned to face her. "What is that?"

"Humans eat fish." Avery shrugged. "They use this tool to catch them. They put something tasty on the hook, drop it down into the water, and wait for a hungry fish."

"Oh, that sounds awful." Bethany winced.

"We all know the way of the ocean." Avery looked from one of her friends to the other. "We're all part of the food chain at some point. No, it's not something I want to think about, but humans have to survive too."

"That's true." Bethany nodded. "I just wonder if *we're* on their food chain."

"That's a good question." Kira swam down toward the collection of items. "They seem to revere some animals." She picked up a statue of a small cat. "Look at this. They've made a statue out of this hideous creature." She pointed to its puffy tail. "Have you ever seen anything like this?"

"It is creepy." Trina cringed.

"I think it's kind of cute." Bethany took the statue from Kira. "It looks like it would be soft."

"Maybe." Kira set the statue down. "But if they revere some animals, then maybe they're not the monsters we imagine them to be."

"Maybe not." Bethany smiled.

"Would you be interested in joining us if we are able to go on a trip to discover more about the humans?" Avery swam over to her. "I think your curiosity would help us out a lot."

"I think so too." Kira nodded.

"If the queen approves it, we might be leaving as soon as tomorrow!" Trina wiggled her tail. "Are you up for it?"

"Absolutely." Bethany splashed her tail through the water. "Oh, I hope she says yes!"

"Don't get too wound up." Kira shook her head. "I doubt that she's going to go for it. Michelle was in so much danger last time, and I think she mentioned that we all broke the surface. The queen is going to be hesitant to let Michelle leave her sight again."

"There's only one way to find out." Avery swam up out of the secret room. She heard her friends swim after her. "Michelle has probably already spoken to the queen by now." She glanced back at her friends. "Remember, we need to be on our best behavior so we can prove to her that we can be trusted to do this."

Bethany's eyes widened. "Avery, we should probably—"

"Bethany, listen, if we want to make this happen, we need to be ready to take orders and follow directions." She looked over at Kira and Trina. "Can we all agree to that?"

"Avery, just listen—"

"No, Trina, I need you to listen. The queen is no pushover. She'll take some convincing. We have to show her that we're a good team or she's going to laugh us all out of the palace."

"Avery!" Kira snapped her tail. "Turn around!"

"Huh?" Avery turned around. She found Queen Maris right behind her. "Your majesty." She bowed. "I'm so sorry, I didn't realize that you were there."

"It's quite alright, Avery." The queen smiled as she looked at her. "I was on my way to find you, actually. I'm surprised to find you down here. You wouldn't have been in the secret room, would you?"

"Uh—yes." Avery cleared her throat. "We were."

"Avery!" Bethany poked her side.

"I just want you to know that you can trust us, Queen Maris. We will always tell you the truth."

"Michelle told me that you wanted to put together a team to find out more about the human world." The queen eyed each of them in turn. "I suppose this wasn't just her idea? My guess is that someone else came up with it?"

"It was me." Avery swam a little closer to her. "I thought it would be a good idea for us to get to know more about the humans—so that we can be prepared if they ever do find out about us."

"That's exactly what Michelle said." The queen looked over the gathered mermaids again, then looked straight into Avery's eyes. "She insisted that it would be wiser than trying to conceal the fact that we exist."

"It does seem that way to me." Avery bit into her bottom lip. Having the queen's full attention on her left her feeling unsettled.

"Interesting idea you've come up with." The queen nodded. "Of course I told Michelle absolutely not." She snapped her tail through the water, sending a ripple toward the entire group of mermaids.

CHAPTER 4

"Oh, I see." Avery nodded. "I understand, Queen Maris. I'm sure that you have your reasons."

"Yes, I do. She's a princess. It's important that she is around to protect all the mermaids. Sending her out on a mission like this is risky and she has important duties to fulfill here."

"Yes, of course." Avery did her best to hold in her disappointment. She wanted to argue. She wanted to explain why she thought it would be a good idea for them to learn more about the humans. However, she respected the queen and didn't want to upset her by questioning her decision.

"That's why I told her that she would not be joining the rest of you." The queen looked over the mermaids before her. "I want you to understand that I value each of you and that you will be at risk as well if you decide to do this. Each of you may decide if you want to participate or not."

"Wait, you mean we can still go?" Avery's eyes widened. "As a team?"

"Yes." The queen smiled. "I think it's a good idea to learn as much as we can about the humans. Certainly, we can't just assume that they are our enemies. It's important to find out whether there is a possibility of mermaids and humans co-existing at some point. Obviously, at this time, we don't want the humans to know about us, but if they happen to discover us, we may have to forge a relationship with them. Knowing as much as we can about them would give us an advantage."

Avery nodded her head as the queen continued looking at each of the mermaids in turn.

"There are real risks that you will face. Not only is the ocean full of dangerous creatures, but the closer you get to land, the closer you will be to humans. Michelle told me that each of you has broken the surface." She frowned. "I have broken the surface as well. It is hard to resist doing it again. But you must resist it at all costs. The only place any of you are safe is in the water."

"We will." Avery's skin buzzed with excitement. "We will be so very careful. I promise, Queen Maris. I know that I want to go, what about the rest of you?" She turned to look at her friends.

"Absolutely." Bethany nodded.

"Me too!" Trina waved her hand through the water.

"And you, Kira?" The queen met Kira's eyes.

"I think so." Kira nodded. "Yes."

"Are you sure?" Queen Maris swam over to her. "I want you to know that you don't have to say yes."

"I won't say that I'm not frightened, but I still want to go. I want to find out everything there is to know about the human world." Kira nodded.

"Okay, then it's settled." The queen looked over the group of mermaids. "Michelle will help you prepare for your journey and of course Bernard will join you." She smiled.

"Bernard?" Avery's tail drooped at the thought. "Does he have to?"

"Yes. Bernard is trained to be a guard, a protector. The only way I will agree to this is if he goes with you." She crossed her arms. "Is that going to be a problem?"

"No, of course not." Avery lowered her eyes. Did the queen know that she was lying?

"I do hope that you will all be able to get along, as teamwork is very important." The queen met the eyes of each of them, then swam off through the water.

"This is terrible." Avery sighed as she drifted against a wall of coral. "I can't believe that Bernard has to go with us."

"It's not so bad, is it?" Kira shrugged. "It's good for us to have someone with us to protect us."

"But Bernard?" Avery moaned. "He's so bossy."

"You just think that because he's your brother." Bethany smiled. "He's not so bad, really."

"Then you must not know him well." Avery rolled her eyes. "I guess we'd better get ready to go."

She swam out of the Coral Palace with her friends in a line behind her.

"Avery!" Michelle waved to her as she swam over. "My mother was looking for you—did she find you?"

"Yes, she told us the news." Avery frowned. "I'm so sorry you won't be able to join us, Michelle."

"That's alright, I understand why I can't. Besides, my mother put me in charge of making sure you all have everything you need. I'm already putting together survival packs for each of you and Bernard." She winced. "I know that part probably wasn't the best news."

"I guess we'll have to find a way to work together." Avery shrugged. "I'm glad you're the one that is putting everything together. When do you think we can leave?"

"I'd say by this afternoon—if you're all okay with that." She looked past Avery at the other mermaids.

"Ready!" Trina nodded.

"I just need to gather a few things!" Bethany swam off.

"Michelle, can I help you with the packs?" Kira met her eyes.

"Sure you can. Thanks." Michelle and Kira swam off together.

"Are you sure about this, Avery?" Trina looked over at her. "Do you really think you can work with Bernard?"

"I'm going to have to find a way." Avery nodded. "In fact, I'll go make sure he's ready right now." She smiled at Trina. "Thanks for joining in, Trina. With the crew we have, I'm sure that we'll be able to discover some amazing new things about the human world."

"Me too." Trina grinned, then swam off through the water.

Avery gritted her teeth. She and her brother Bernard had never gotten along, but she was determined to make this work. If that meant she had to be as nice as she could to him, then that was what she would do. The question was, could he do the same for her?

CHAPTER 5

Avery searched everywhere for her brother. She looked in all his favorite places. She checked with the other guards that he usually spent time with. There was no sign of him.

Frustrated, she headed back toward the Coral Palace to meet up with her friends.

When she arrived, Michelle was there with packs for each of them and another pack meant for Bernard.

"There you are, Avery." Michelle smiled. "I was about to send out a search party to find you."

"Sorry, I was looking for Bernard." She frowned as her brother swam right up to the group.

"I'll bet you were." He crossed his arms.

"Bernard, where have you been?" Avery stared at him.

"Hiding from you. I didn't want to hear you complain about my assignment." He took his pack from Michelle. "Are we ready to go?"

Avery fumed as she took her pack. She snapped her fingers and the pack disappeared. She knew she would be able to get it back with another snap of her fingers. For now, it was safely tucked away until she needed it. Already she felt as if Bernard was making things difficult. She just hoped he wouldn't cause her to lose the chance to lead the team.

"I think we're all ready." She glanced over at her friends. "Does everyone have everything they need?"

"We're ready when you are." Bethany grinned. "I can't wait!"

"Remember." Michelle looked at Bethany. "All of you must come back unharmed. If my mother believes that she put any of you in danger, she won't let this continue. Now, the assignment is to journey close to land, but not to take any risk of being seen. You may collect any human created objects you find, but do not try to use them until they've been brought back to the palace to be examined. Do you all understand?"

"Yes, we do." Avery's heart began to pound. She was excited to get started too. It meant a lot to her that Queen Maris had enough trust in them to carry this assignment out. "Let's go!" She smiled at her friends.

"I'll lead the way." Bernard swam off ahead.

Avery frowned as the others swam after him.

"Avery, wait." Michelle caught her hand. "Listen, I know it's going to be hard for you to work with Bernard, but he has been given special training and he can keep you safe."

"I know." Avery nodded. "I'll do my best to get along with him."

"Good." Michelle snapped her fingers. A necklace appeared in her palm with one gem on it. "My mother made this for you—to make sure that you could find your way back." She put it over Avery's head. "Please be careful. And Avery, I want to know every detail!"

"I will be, and I promise I will remember everything!" She hugged Michelle, then swam off after the others.

It took quite some time for them to get close to land. Every now and then Bernard would wave his hand through the water and a glow would form in front of him.

"What is that?" Avery tried to swim close enough to see it.

"Nothing you need to know about." He scowled and waved his hand, which made the glow disappear.

"Bernard, please. We need to work together. Right now we have to forget about being brother and sister."

"You would like that, wouldn't you?" He raised an eyebrow. "Forget it Avery. Just listen to what I tell you and we'll get through this fine."

"Bernard, I'm supposed to be leading this team." Avery frowned.

"Team?" He laughed as the others gathered around them. "You're a bunch of kids. The only reason the queen agreed to this is because she wants you to learn that humans are to be feared."

"That's not true." Bethany crossed her arms. "Queen Maris wants us to learn more about them."

"Yes, she does. She wants you to learn that they are monsters." He looked at each of them in turn. "Since none of you have figured that out yet, she's worried that you'll go off and get yourself captured by one of those creatures. So she asked me to go along with you to make sure that you don't do anything foolish like last time."

"I knew it was a terrible idea for you to come with us." Avery put her hands on her hips. "You're lying, Bernard! You hate humans, so you want us to hate them too!"

"Yes I hate them!" Bernard slapped his hand through the water, which made all the other mermaids float backward from the force. "They are terrible creatures! If they find out about us, they will hunt us down! They don't have hearts like we do!"

"I don't believe that." Trina swam forward.

"How can you say that?" Bernard groaned. "After what you

saw? What do you think, Carlos?" He stared at the lobster on Kira's shoulder. "Do you think humans want to be our friends? You saw lobsters just like you trapped in cages. Are you curious to learn more about humans?"

"I just want to make sure we're all safe." Carlos smiled. "I've met a lot of lobsters I'm not fond of and I've met a lot of lobsters that I am fond of. I can't say that every lobster is the same, so I don't think the same could be said for humans. They are alive, just like us, aren't they?"

"Maybe." Bernard shrugged. "Maybe not. We don't even know that much about them, do we?"

"Which is why we're on this mission." Kira spoke up and reached up to pet Carlos's claw. "If we're not brave enough to find out the truth about humans, then who will be?" She looked straight at Bernard. "Are you going to be brave with us so we can complete our mission or are you going to fight us every step of the way?"

CHAPTER 6

"You'll never have to ask me to be brave." Bernard huffed. "It's my nature to be brave. But it's not my nature to be foolish. Yes, we need to learn about humans, but not so we can take one home as a cute little pet. You get that, don't you, Avery?" He raised an eyebrow.

"Of course I do. I would never want a human as a pet." Avery crossed her arms.

"That's what you said about that poisonous sea snail—oh, and the sea turtle. Remember that? You hid it in your shell until it was so big it could have eaten you in one bite!" He shook his head.

"Tommy never would have hurt me—or anyone!" She scowled. "If it wasn't for you telling on me, he'd still be with me. Instead, I had to release him into the deep sea." She sniffled. "I hope he's okay."

"I'm sure he is—because he's a wild creature, Avery. That's the problem, you always think that these creatures are cute and harmless. But they're not. They're trying to survive, just like the rest of us, and they aren't safe to have as pets. Tommy might have been cute when you first found him, but that doesn't mean he wouldn't have attacked you at some point."

"You can't know that." She put her hands on her hips.

"And you can't know that he wouldn't have." Bernard swam right in front of her and looked her in the eye. "Avery, you are my little sister and I will do what it takes to protect you, even if that means protecting you from yourself." He ruffled her hair. "Now, let's go." He turned to swim away.

"No." Avery crossed her arms. She looked over at her friends then back to her brother. "Not until you tell me what you have in your hand."

"Fine." He rolled his eyes as he looked back at her. "It's a map." He held out his hand to reveal a small pebble. "The queen gave it to me. It shows us where the land is, so we don't spend days swimming in a circle looking for it. It also warns us when we're getting too close." He closed his hand over the pebble. "She trusted me to guide you all on this mission. Maybe you should start trusting me too." He glared at Avery, then looked at the other mermaids. "I'm here to help you. Whether you like it or not, I'm not going anywhere." He began to swim again.

Avery frowned as she swam behind him.

"That just might be the coolest thing ever." Bethany swam up beside her. "I didn't even know something like that existed. It's not too different from the necklace that Michelle has."

"I have a piece of it now." Avery showed her the necklace she wore. "They are both pretty amazing."

"Yes, they are." Bethany frowned, then lowered her voice. "But where did they come from? They don't look like human tools. They look like things found in our world, but they have some kind of magic."

"I don't know much about them." Avery shrugged. "I guess they are things mermaids have created on their own."

"I've never met a magical mermaid, have you?" Bethany swam even closer to her. "Do you think Queen Maris is magical? Maybe she charmed the pebble and the gems."

"I don't know." Avery frowned. "It's not important right now. We need to find out what we can about humans, not about magical mermaids."

"You're right." Bethany fell a short distance behind Avery, then she swam swiftly up beside her again. "Avery, do you ever feel like there's so much we don't know?"

"All of the time, especially since I've learned about humans."

"I feel like our parents, or at least the queen—they know more about everything than what they tell us. Like we only get half the story."

"Maybe that's true." Avery looked over at her. "But maybe they have their reasons for only sharing what they do." She winced. "Maybe there are things we would rather not know."

"Maybe." Bethany shook her head. "But I want to know everything—everything there is to know."

"Then let's start with this." Avery smiled at her. "Let's see if we can catch up to Bernard. He's having a little too much fun being in charge."

"Good idea." Bethany laughed as she charged forward through the water.

Avery swished her tail swiftly as she chased after her.

Kira and Trina bolted after the two of them.

"Wait up!" Trina laughed.

"Slow down!" Carlos gulped as he clung onto Kira's hair.

Soon the mermaids swarmed around Bernard.

He spun around in the water and snapped his tail at them.

"Don't swim so fast, you'll make waves and attract predators." He scowled at them. "Look at all the bubbles you're making!"

"We're just having fun, Bernard!" Avery laughed. "How much farther until land?"

"Let me check." He opened his palm and a glow spread out across the water in front of him. It projected a topographical map, a map of all the land nearby. "We're not far." He started to close his hand, then froze. He stared through the glow at a giant pair of eyes. The eyes belonged to a giant body, a body that spread so far and wide it was hard to see where it ended. The top of it rounded all the way toward the surface of the water. Its belly rested in the sand below them. "A whale," Bernard whispered as his entire body shuddered. "Get back!" he hissed to the others. "Slowly and quietly, get back!"

Avery stared at the giant creature. She watched as it began to open its enormous mouth. In one bite, it could not only eat one of them, it could eat all of them!

CHAPTER 7

Avery grabbed Trina's hand and started to pull her back away from Bernard and the whale. Kira inched backwards as well, very slowly.

The mammoth creature's mouth opened further, then a cry vibrated the water that surrounded the mermaids.

"It's going to eat us, it's going to eat us!" Kira squeezed her eyes shut.

"Oh no!" Bethany swam up beside Bernard.

"Bethany, get back!" he hissed at her.

"Shh." Bethany stared straight at the whale. "She's not going to hurt us."

"What are you talking about?" Bernard growled. "She's trying to swallow us whole!"

"No, she's crying." Bethany swam forward beyond Bernard and closer to the whale.

"Bethany, no!" Avery swam forward as well and grabbed her friend's arm. "Don't get so close!"

"Look!" Bethany pointed to the sand the whale sprawled across. "She's stuck in the shallow water. She can't move!" She pulled her arm free and swam right up to the whale. "You poor little thing, you've probably been stuck here for days!"

"Little thing?" Bernard's eyes widened. "I'm not sure I trust your judgment if you call that little, Bethany!"

"Wait, she's right." Avery swam closer to the whale as well. "There's not enough water for her to move." She trailed her fingertips along the whale's smooth surface. "She's stuck."

"Doesn't that mean she's probably very hungry?" Kira peered around Trina's shoulder.

"I think so," Bea squeaked as she hid in Trina's hair. "She's probably happy the snacks have arrived!"

"Don't be so hasty!" Carlos swam away from Kira toward the whale. "The waters have been changing so much lately—getting warmer in cold places and colder in warm places—that these big creatures can get confused. She probably thought she was going toward the deep water. Didn't you?" He looked into the whale's eyes.

The whale's large mouth opened again. Another cry escaped. This one was so loud that Bethany and Avery were pushed back away from the whale by the vibrations.

"She's weak," Trina murmured. "She can't even talk." She swam over to the whale and stroked her head. "It's okay, we'll help you."

"Help her?" Bernard threw his hands up through the water. "Help her how?" He looked around at the other mermaids. "In case you've missed it, she's far larger than all of us put together. How exactly do you think we can help her?"

"I'm not sure yet." Avery frowned. "But we have to try."

"We had an assignment, remember?" Bernard shook his head. "And it didn't involve whale rescue."

"Queen Maris would never leave this poor creature here to die." Avery shot a stern look at him. "How do you think she would feel if she found out that you did?"

"It's not like I want her to die!" Bernard huffed. "It's just not possible for us to do anything about it!"

"There's always a way to help." Carlos clacked his claws. "We just need to get her into the deeper water, then she'll be free."

"Yes, free to eat us!" Kira swam over to Bernard. "Bernard is right. We have no idea what she will do once she's free. She probably is very hungry and she will need to fill her belly."

"I don't care." Avery narrowed her eyes. "I'm going to help her. No one else has to, but I'm not leaving her."

"Me either." Bethany floated close to the whale. "She needs us."

"Maybe we could try digging the sand out from under her?" Trina began to dig handfuls of sand out from under the whale. "If we can dig deep, she might sink far enough to be able to swim forward."

"That will take days!" Bernard shook his head. "Even if we had that kind of time, I doubt the whale would survive that long. What we need to do is move her ourselves."

"That's a good idea, Bernard." Avery smiled as she met his eyes. "Does that mean you're going to help us?"

"What choice do I have?" He frowned. "I'm here to protect you. I can't just stand aside and let you get swallowed whole."

"We need to have a plan for when we do get her free." Kira swished her tail through the water. "If we push her from behind and get her to move forward, then we should be fairly safe because we'll be in the shallow water where she got stuck in the first place."

"Brilliant." Bernard nodded and briefly met Kira's eyes. Then he looked back at the whale. "The only problem is, we're not going to be able to budge her."

"We can't know that unless we try!" Avery swam to the back of the whale.

Bethany and Trina followed after her.

"It's plain to see, Avery!" Bernard swam after her too with Kira right behind him. "She's far larger than all of us, which means she's stronger than all of us. Even our combined strength couldn't move her an inch!"

"That doesn't mean we can't try!" Avery placed her hands against the whale. Her friends did the same. Bernard shook his head, then added his strength to the collective push.

Avery closed her eyes tight and pushed as hard as she could. The whale didn't move. Not even a little bit. When Avery opened her eyes all of her friends were looking at her.

"What now?" Trina frowned.

"If we can't push her, maybe we can pull her?" Kira tipped her head to the side.

"That would put us right near her mouth. No way!" Bernard crossed his arms. "There's nothing we can do."

"We need something stronger." Avery frowned. "Something bigger." She looked over at her brother.

"We need Tommy." Bernard put his fingers between his lips and blew hard. A shriek carried through the water.

CHAPTER 8

"Bernard? What are you doing?" Avery's eyes widened.

"I couldn't just let him go into the deep ocean." Bernard frowned. "I loved Tommy too, you know. I used to play with him while you were off with your friends. I've kept track of him and made sure he had enough to eat and that he's safe."

The water ahead of them darkened as a giant turtle swam toward them.

"Big, big turtle!" Kira squeaked and ducked behind Trina.

"Wow!" Bethany's eyes widened. "I didn't even know they could get that big!"

"Tommy is the biggest I've ever seen." Bernard smiled.

"Tommy?" Avery spread her arms wide and swam toward the turtle.

"Avery?" Tommy dipped his big head and peered at her. "It's really you!"

"Oh, Tommy, I was so worried about you." She did her best to wrap her arms around his neck. "You've grown so much!"

"So have you." Tommy smiled. Then he looked at Bernard. "Did you call me?"

"I did." Bernard tipped his head toward the whale. "Do you think you could give us a hand here?"

"Oh, Gladys, not again." Tommy shook his head. "She gets a little confused sometimes. Let me help." He swam around behind the whale.

All of the mermaids joined together with Tommy and gave Gladys a hard push.

Gladys inched forward. After another hard shove, she slid right off of the sand and into the deep water.

The sudden movement made all of the mermaids tumble and spin through the water.

Gladys opened her wide mouth as she turned toward them.

"Oh no!" Kira gulped.

"Eek!" Carlos hid in her hair.

"It's all over!" Bea slid down Trina's shoulder to her arm.

"It's okay." Trina scooped Bea up in her hands and held her close.

"Get back!" Bernard jumped in front of all of them. "Harpoon!" He snapped his fingers.

"Listen!" Bethany grabbed Bernard's arm before he could summon a weapon.

The water pulsed all around them with a slow, deep sound.

"She's singing." Avery whispered. She smiled as she stared at the whale. "She's saying thank you."

"You're welcome, Gladys!" Trina grinned and waved at the whale.

Gladys turned and swam off through the water.

"Thanks for your help, Tommy." Avery patted his wide flipper. "I've missed you so much."

"I've missed you too." Tommy smiled. "I have to go now, but if you ever need me, just whistle."

"I'll teach you how." Bernard swam over to Avery. "It's not too hard."

"Thanks." Avery looked at her brother for a moment. Maybe he wasn't so bad after all. "Thank you for looking after Tommy too." She hugged him.

"Alright, enough." Bernard pushed her away and laughed. "We still have a job to do, remember?"

"Yes, we do." Kira looked up at the sunlight that sparkled through the shallow water. "We're better off getting closer while the sun is still out."

"Wait, before we go, I need to remind all of you, as the water gets more shallow the chance of breaking the surface goes up. We need to be careful. No breaking the surface! Understand?" He looked from each of them to the other.

"Yes, we understand." Avery rolled her eyes. "We all know the rules. Let's go!" She swam toward the more shallow water.

The closer she got to land, the warmer the water became. It was a temperature she'd never experienced in the deeper water. She glanced back at her friends, who all swam close to her.

Bernard hung back a short distance. His eyes darted back and forth in search of any predators.

She turned back toward the shallow water and was startled by something that she had never seen before. Four hairy legs were swimming toward her. She lifted her head enough to see the bottom half of the creature. As it swam closer to her, she backed up and signaled for her friends to do the same.

"What is that thing?" Trina shuddered. "It's like a big hairy crab."

A sharp whistle echoed through the water. The hairy legs thrashed through the water, then spun around and swam toward land.

"There must be humans nearby." Bernard swam closer to them. "Let's go back to the deeper water."

"No, Bernard!" Avery caught him by the arm. "Isn't that

why we're here?" She tugged him forward. When she felt him tremble, she looked back at him. "Bernard, are you scared?"

"Of course not." He jerked his arm free. "We need to think this through. We don't even know what that creature in the water was. What if it saw us?"

"With what? Its legs?" Avery shook her head. "It didn't see us. This is perfect. We might get to know what that other creature is, but only if we get closer." Her voice softened. "Bernard, it's okay if you're scared. We're all a little scared. As long as we stick together, we're going to be just fine. Alright?" She offered her hand to him.

"Okay, fine. But stay close to me." He swam forward with a snap of his tail.

Avery swam after him. It still surprised her that her tough big brother could be so frightened of humans. Yes, her heart skipped a beat at the thought of seeing one, but he seemed more frightened than she was.

The mermaids swam together as a group toward the land. Bernard steered them away from the beach and along a line of rocks that jutted out. It provided a small pool of deeper water and a safe place for them to observe.

As Avery clung to the rocks with her head just below the surface, she felt the urge to break through. She wanted to see what was happening on the beach. She wanted to know what that creature was that had swum toward them.

As the top of her head brushed against the surface, she heard a loud sharp sound echo through the water. It made her jump and a second later she felt air against her forehead.

CHAPTER 9

Avery's eyes widened as she realized she had broken the surface right up to the tip of her nose.

Before she could sink back down, the furry-legged creature made a loud sound again—only outside of the water, it was much louder and much sharper. It rang through her ears even though they were still half under the water. Its strange face neared hers, took a deep breath through its dark nostrils, and then it began to make the noise over and over again.

She shivered. There was no question that she had been spotted. If she slipped back under the water, would it come after her? She had no idea what to expect.

It ran back and forth along the rocks and continued to make that horrible sound. Then she heard another sound—a more familiar sound.

A human's voice shouted, "Baxter, enough with the barking! We're at the beach, it can't be that serious!"

The voice got closer with every word spoken. In seconds, a human would see her.

Frozen with fear, she felt a sharp tug on her tail.

Seconds later she plunged back down under the water,

though not by her choice. Bernard's arms were wrapped tight around her waist and held her down beneath the surface.

"Avery, are you okay?"

"I think so." She shivered again. "The creature is right above us—and a human as well."

"Did they see you?" He looked up through the water.

"No, the human didn't. The creature did." She scrunched up her nose. "It sniffed me."

"Oh no!" Kira clapped her hands over her mouth.

"Gross." Trina shuddered.

"Is it cute?" Bethany peered up at the surface.

"It's...strange." Avery frowned. "The human said it was barking. I don't think it speaks their language. I don't think it will be able to tell them anything."

"You don't think? You keep saying that." Bernard scowled. "But you don't know! Do you?"

"No, I don't." She snapped her tail through the water. "I didn't mean to break the surface, Bernard! I heard that loud noise and it made me jump and then I was just out. But now I know how we can watch the humans."

"How?" Bethany swam over to her.

"As long as we keep our mouth and nose under the water, we can still breathe just fine. Just the tops of our heads will be out of the water—just enough for us to see what they are up to."

"That's still breaking the surface." Bernard crossed his arms.

"Yes, I know it is." Avery looked at him impatiently. "How else can we learn anything about them?"

"It's risky." Kira shook her head. "The creature sniffed you this time, but next time it could be a human."

"Ugh, gross." Trina waved her hand in front of her face. "Could you imagine a human getting that close? They're so weird."

"What's so weird about them?" Bethany rolled her eyes. "The only real difference I can see between humans and us is that we have tails and they have legs. They have two eyes, a nose, and a mouth. They have the same language." She swam toward the surface of the water. "What if humans aren't a different species? What if they're some kind of mermaid?" She glanced back at the others.

"That's ridiculous." Bernard laughed.

"Is it?" Avery swam closer to Bethany. "She's right. They look a lot like us."

"So what?" Kira frowned. "That doesn't make them the same as us. They are murderers, remember?"

"We don't know that for sure." Avery looked back at her brother. "That's why we have to find out more. If it means breaking the surface, then that is what we have to do."

"Avery! You heard what the queen said!" Bernard glared at her.

"I heard her, yes. But I don't want to go back to Eldoris with a story about furry legs and a sniff, do you?" She looked back at the surface of the water. "They're out there, right out there for us to see. Why can't we just take a look?"

"I'll tell you why." Bernard narrowed his eyes and crossed his arms. "Because I said so."

"Is that the best you've got?" Trina giggled.

"Seriously." He looked at each of them in turn. "Queen Maris trusted you and told you to listen to me."

"Yes, you're right, she did." Avery swam back down toward him. "Now I'm asking you, Bernard, as brave as you are, don't you think there is a way we can do this without any humans seeing us? Think of all the information we could report back with. Think of all the good it would do."

"It can't really hurt." Kira nodded. "Not just a quick look. What are they going to see? The tops of our heads, like Avery said? We do look very similar to humans. They won't even think twice about it if they do see us."

"Exactly." Bethany smiled.

"It still seems like a bad idea." Bernard winced.

"Look at it this way, Bernard. Do you want to go back to the queen and tell her that none of us listened to you, that you can't be trusted to babysit your little sister and her friends? Or are you going to go back and say that you made a choice that you thought was best?" Trina put her hands on her hips as she looked at Bernard. "Because you can't stop us from breaking the surface if that's what we decide to do."

"You four are impossible!" Bernard shouted and thrashed his hands through the water. The sudden swish of water elevated him right to the surface and a second later, he broke through it.

"He did it!" Avery laughed. "He broke the surface!" She swam up beside him, as did the other three mermaids.

One by one, they each pushed the tops of their heads through the surface of the water.

CHAPTER 10

Relieved to see that the barking creature was gone, Avery looked toward the beach.

The sun had begun to set, but there were a few humans that walked along the water. One was tall, one was short, and one was tiny.

She stared at the tiny one that toddled forward, her fingers curled around the tallest human's hands. The shorter human splashed at the edge of the water. He ran back and forth and laughed. Yes, it was laughter, only it sounded different than it did under the water. It made her want to spin and dance. But she resisted.

A quick look over at Bernard revealed that he had his attention focused on her and the other mermaids.

She looked back at the humans. As she watched, the short human splashed the water high into the air. It drenched the tiny human. The tiny human threw back her head and a terrible sound escaped her.

Avery winced as the high-pitched screech struck her ears. Bernard sank down beneath the water. So did Kira and Trina.

Avery forced herself to stay. She reached for the hand of Bethany, who also remained above the water.

As they watched, the tallest human scooped the tiny human up into her arms and cradled it close against her chest. The shriek stopped. The tiny human wrapped her arms around the tallest human's neck.

Avery's heart pounded as she realized what she'd seen.

She sank back down under the water, along with Bethany.

"They have mothers," she blurted out.

"They have babies." Bethany's eyes widened.

"Yes, they definitely have babies." Bernard winced and shook his head. "I can remember when you screamed like that, Avery. It was awful."

"I didn't scream like that!" Avery crossed her arms.

"How would you know? You were a baby." He glared at her.

"Okay, listen, this changes everything." Bethany held up her hands. "It shows that these aren't just wild creatures that want to consume other creatures. They have families—like we do."

"You don't know that." Bernard shook his head. "You don't know that they are a family. They could just be a few humans grouped together."

"I know that one of them was the big brother." Avery smirked. "Because he splashed the baby and made it scream!"

"That's a good point." Kira grinned.

"It's not funny." Bernard looked up toward the surface. "All this means is that there are going to be more of them, lots more of them. It makes things even more dangerous for us."

"Maybe not." Bethany tipped her head to the side. "Maybe it means that they know what love is. If they know what loves is, then they must feel compassion, right?"

"I think you're right." Carlos scuttled across the sand in the shallow water.

"Even after what you said before, Carlos?" Kira looked down at him.

"Yes. It's not like only humans eat us lobsters. Lots of creatures eat us. But the way that mother held her baby—it says a lot about what kind of creatures humans are." He hummed softly. "It reminds me of my mother and the songs she would sing to me."

"Even if there are some humans that are like that, it certainly doesn't mean that they are all like that." Bernard frowned as the last of the sunlight disappeared. "We'd better get back. Do we have enough to report back to the queen now, Avery? Or are you going to trick me into breaking the surface again?"

"I didn't trick you." Avery huffed. "You got so mad that you shot right out of the water. That wasn't my fault."

"You two." Trina rolled her eyes.

"Cool it," Bea piped up from Trina's shoulder. "The queen didn't send you two here to fight. She sent you here to find out what you could about the humans."

A strong voice spoke up from behind them. "And here I thought that was my job."

"Halt!" Bernard spun around to face the creature.

"Relax, Bernard, it's just Michelle's grandfather." Avery smiled. "It's good to see you again, sir."

"Thank you. Please, call me Ben." He swam closer to the other mermaids. "Maris told me that you would be on this mission. She asked me to keep an eye on all of you, to make sure that she could trust you."

Avery's heart sank. She'd had no idea that they were being watched. Now the queen would know that they had defied her order not to break the surface. She would certainly never trust them again.

"I can explain." She frowned.

"No need." Ben shrugged. "I knew you wouldn't be able to learn anything about the humans without breaking the surface. You came up with a safe way to explore. I guess you could say that you passed the test." He looked amongst the lot of them. "You figured out how to put your differences aside for the good of the mission. Now I know that you're serious enough to learn about the humans." He raised an eyebrow. "And now you know that they are not all terrifying creatures." He tipped his head toward the surface. "They're not so different from us, it's true. But they also can't be trusted. They fear what is different from them and they panic when they discover something new." He frowned. "I had hoped that we would be able to make a connection with them, but so far my attempts have been disastrous. Perhaps some young mermaids like yourselves will be able to come up with some new ideas." He looked at each of them for a long moment. "There is something I'd like to give you, but I need to know that you are going to be extremely careful with it. Can I trust you? All of you?"

"Yes sir." Bernard nodded.

"Yes, absolutely." Avery smiled as her heart quickened with excitement. "What is it?"

"You can trust us, Ben." Kira perked up as she swam closer to Trina.

"Sure you can." Trina nodded. "We make a great team."

"And you?" He looked straight at Bethany. "Can I trust you, Bethany?"

"You know my name?" Her eyes widened.

"I worked with your mother before, you know. She taught me a lot about the human world." He smiled. "I was excited to hear that you would be part of this mission. But I still need to know, can I trust you?"

"Yes, of course you can." Bethany stared at him.

"Good. Then I will give you a tool that only I have used

before." He snapped his fingers and five gems appeared in the palm of his hand.

"Oh, shiny!" Trina reached for one.

"Careful." He pulled his hand back. "They aren't toys. Once you place one of these on your neck, it will attach to your skin and allow you to breathe and speak outside of the water. But if you leave it on too long, you will lose the ability to breathe underwater again. You must only use them when you absolutely have to."

"That sounds terrible." Kira swam back away from his hand.

"It is quite a risk." He nodded. "But I trust that you'll be very careful. It will give you a chance to breathe the air. But breathing too much of it can make you dependent on it." He held his hand out to them. "You can each choose one. Once you do, it will be yours and only yours. Don't lose it, as there are very few of these that exist."

"How do they exist?" Bethany stared into his eyes. "Did you create them?"

"That is a story for another day." He smiled as each mermaid chose a gem. "Now go back home and tell the queen what I've given you. She will know that you have done a good job." He glanced up at the surface, then back to them. "I can only hope that you will be able to find a way to connect with the humans in a way that I haven't been able to. The future of Eldoris depends on it."

BOOK 5: BETHANY

CHAPTER 1

A billowing cloud of bubbles floated past Bethany as a school of fish splashed through the water. She watched the smooth movement of the creatures and found peace in it.

Under the water, everything was fairly predictable. She had studied so many of the creatures that lived in the sea, as well as the plants, the patterns of currents, and even the tides. But beyond the water—where land stretched as far as the eye could see—was a great mystery to her. A mystery that Bethany desperately wanted to solve.

She closed her eyes as she recalled the things she'd seen on her recent journeys with her friends. Just a few months ago, it had never even occurred to her to try to communicate with humans. But now, it was the only thing she could think about.

These were new creatures, perhaps not so different from mermaids, that could teach and share knowledge that she couldn't even dream of discovering on her own. Why wouldn't everyone want to communicate with them?

She'd been eager to get back out and explore, but there was a rumble of fear throughout the mermaid community. The gems that they'd been given scared many of her friends. The thought of not being able to breathe under the water was too great a risk. Each of them had tucked their gem away and gone back to living their normal lives. But Bethany couldn't shake the urge to see and speak to humans. The gem would give her the opportunity to not only breathe air, but to speak to a human, to know once and for all whether they were murderous creatures or not so different from mermaids.

"Bethany!"

Startled by the sound of her mother's voice, she looked away from the fish and turned in the direction of the small home they shared. Her mother swam out through the front door and waved to her. As her long hair billowed around her, Bethany stared at her.

Her mother was an expert on humans, something Bethany hadn't known until the queen's brother had recently revealed the truth to her. She knew that her mother studied many things, but until that moment, she'd had no idea how much study she'd devoted to humans.

Now Bethany saw her mother a little differently. She was no longer just a loving mermaid who always made sure Bethany's hair was untangled and her belly was full. She was a mysterious being that held many secrets about the great beyond.

"I'm here, Mom." Bethany swam over to her.

"You've been out for hours. Have you eaten at all?" Her mother swept some of Bethany's hair back away from her face. "Why aren't you spending time with your friends?"

"I was just studying the fish." She met her mother's eyes. "I wonder how they are impacted by the fishing activities of the humans."

"The humans." Her mother crossed her arms and rolled her eyes. "That's all I hear about from you anymore."

"I'm just so curious." Bethany frowned.

"It's alright." Her mother smiled as she cupped her daughter's chin and looked into her eyes. "I know what curiosity is like."

"Then you should tell me everything you know," Bethany pleaded. "Mom, why won't you tell me about your studies of the humans?"

"Because it's not important." Her mother glanced away. "All you need to know is that they are dangerous creatures. Interesting, yes. Wonderful, maybe. But dangerous, absolutely." She caught Bethany's hand and gave it a firm squeeze. "Queen Maris was right to declare that you all should take a break from your adventures. The lure of the humans can be so strong that you will end up taking risks that you know you shouldn't. When you are all a little older you can return to exploring, but for now, you should respect the queen's decree and let all this go."

"But I can't, Mom." She sank down in the water as she stared up at her mother. "Can't you understand that?"

"I understand that if I find out you are involved in something with the humans, there will be consequences." She narrowed her eyes. "Bethany, curiosity is a wonderful trait, but sometimes it can lead you astray. You have to be in control of it. Understand?"

"Yes, Mother." Bethany watched as her mother swam away. Most of the time they were very close. She'd learned so much from her. But ever since the queen had announced that their explorers' group would be disbanded, her mother had never seemed more distant from her. It seemed that she was careful about everything she said to Bethany.

Disappointed yet again, Bethany swam toward her room. As she drew close to it, she heard a subtle splash through the water. Then she saw a shadow. Her eyes widened as she realized that there was someone in her room.

It couldn't be her mother; she had just gone in the other

direction. It couldn't be any of her friends; they had been busy with their own lives and hadn't visited her lately. So who was it?

Frightened, she drifted closer to the window. From the size and shape of the creature, she guessed that it had to be another mermaid. But who?

Before she could figure that out, the stranger burst through the window and swam so swiftly past her that the force of the disrupted water knocked her back a few feet.

"Hey! Stop!" she called out to the mermaid, but the mermaid snapped her tail so swiftly that a shower of bubbles disguised her from view. All Bethany managed to see was a cloud of dark hair that swirled through the water as the mermaid made her escape.

"Come back here!" Bethany shouted. Her heart began to pound. What was the mermaid doing in her room? Why was she swimming away so fast?

CHAPTER 2

Bethany chased after the mermaid. But the mermaid swam faster than any other mermaid she'd ever known. In fact, she swam faster than most sea creatures.

Exhausted, Bethany finally gave up and turned back. Her muscles ached from trying to catch up with the other mermaid. She still had no idea who it could be. She knew that there were other mermaids outside of Eldoris, but she didn't often see them.

Most mermaids lived within the safety of Eldoris. A few chose to live in other areas of the sea and didn't have the protection that Eldoris offered. Bethany wasn't sure why a mermaid would choose to live outside of the city. She guessed it was because they didn't want to have to follow the rules that Queen Maris made to keep them safe. Perhaps it wasn't a strange mermaid at all, perhaps it was someone she knew quite well and she just couldn't figure out who it was.

As she swam into her room, she noticed that several of her things floated through the water instead of being tucked into the shelves of the rocky wall that surrounded her bed. Startled, she began to collect her things before they could float away.

There was her collection of shells and her assortment of different kinds of seaweed. She tucked them back into place. What could that mermaid have been looking for? Her heart suddenly sank as she recalled the special gem that she'd been given.

She had tucked it inside a clamshell, which she'd tucked into a conch shell, which she'd wedged under the large shell she slept in. It had to still be there. She was sure it had to be.

She swam down under her shell and felt some relief when she spotted the conch shell. She pulled it out and reached inside. She smiled some as she felt the smooth surface of the clamshell. She pulled it out of the conch shell and opened it. As she stared at the empty space inside, her mind spun. How could it be gone? She had promised to keep it safe, to be very careful with it. It couldn't have floated away. She'd tucked it away so well. Which meant that the mermaid that had been in her room must have taken it.

"Oh no!" She gulped down a big swallow of water as her heart began to race. How would she explain this to the queen? Who could have taken it?

The gems were a secret. Only Queen Maris and a few others in the Coral Palace knew about them. And of course her friends, who'd also each received one. Could it have been one of them who took it? Or told someone else about its being there?

Frightened, she swam out of her room and through the water in the direction of the Coral Palace. She would have to tell the queen right away. It was the right thing to do. However, admitting that she had lost a magical gem—a magical gem that she had been charged with protecting and keeping safe—made her sick to her stomach.

Would Queen Maris ever trust her again?

As she drew closer to the palace, she spotted Avery and Bernard batting a ball of kelp back and forth with their tails.

Would they understand if she told them what had happened? Would they be angry at her?

"Avery!" She waved to her friend.

As Avery turned to look at her, Bernard whacked the ball of kelp hard with his tail and sent it flying. It smacked Avery right in the side of the head.

"Ow! Watch it!" Avery huffed at Bernard.

"Pay attention!" Bernard scowled at her.

"Sorry." Bethany frowned. Already she'd caused trouble.

"It's okay, Bethany." Avery swam over to her. "Where have you been? We've all been a little worried about you."

"Oh, I've been around." Bethany shrugged.

"Not around us." Avery crossed her arms. "Trina thinks you're angry at us for some reason."

"Angry?" Bethany shook her head. "Not at all. I just can't stop thinking about certain things." She bit into her bottom lip.

"Humans?" Avery whispered.

"Yes." Bethany nodded. "I know everyone else wants to forget, so I've been keeping to myself."

"But we don't—we don't want to forget." Avery glanced over her shoulder at her brother, then steered Bethany away from him. "We all want to go back. But after what Queen Maris said, we don't think we'll ever be able to."

"Really?" Bethany's eyes widened. "I had no idea."

"Because you've been avoiding us, Bethany. We're your friends." Avery met her eyes. "You should know you can talk to us about anything. Got it?"

"Thanks." Bethany smiled some. "I didn't know that, but I do now."

"Good." Avery narrowed her eyes. "Now, what's wrong? You look so worried."

All at once Bethany remembered the stolen gem. Avery said she could talk to her about anything, but did that include losing the most important magical gem ever created? Her heart skipped a beat.

"Something terrible has happened, Avery."

"What is it?" Avery took Bethany's hand. "It's okay, Bethany. You can tell me."

Fear bubbled up in Bethany's chest, but she forced herself to admit the truth.

"Someone stole my gem. I tried to catch her, but she was far too fast. The gem is gone and now I have to tell Queen Maris the truth. I can't begin to imagine how angry she will be." She blinked back tears as she looked at Avery. "I don't know what to do. I did my best to hide it away safely, but it was like she knew just where to look for it."

"She? It was another mermaid?" Avery tightened her grasp on Bethany's hand. "Do you know who it was?"

"No." Bethany shook her head. "I've never seen her before."

CHAPTER 3

"Are you sure?" Avery stared into her eyes. "You must know all the mermaids in Eldoris—we all do. Think about it. It must have been someone you knew."

"It wasn't." Bethany frowned. "I couldn't see her face. She had very long dark hair. I don't think there is a mermaid in Eldoris that has hair that long and that dark. It was as long as her tail."

"Wow." Avery shook her head. "No I can't think of anyone with hair like that either. And you're sure she took the gem?"

"It wasn't where I hid it. She must have taken it." Bethany's hands balled into fists. "What am I going to do? When the queen finds out, she'll be so angry. She'll never let me be part of the group again."

"Listen, you couldn't have known that someone would steal it." Avery hugged her. "I'd better go check and make sure that mine is still where I hid it. We need to tell the others too."

"What about Queen Maris?" Bethany swam after her as Avery darted toward her home.

"Don't tell her just yet. Maybe between all of us, we can

figure out a way to get the gem back." She swam off again. "See if you can find Michelle or Trina!"

Bethany shivered at the thought. Michelle would certainly want to tell her mother—the queen—right away. Trina was so strong and brave. She'd likely believe that Bethany could have hidden the gem better or tried harder to protect it.

Instead of looking for either of them, Bethany decided to look for Kira. She guessed that Kira might understand what had happened the best out of all her friends. As she swam through the water, her heart continued to pound. If she didn't find the gem, what would happen? How could she find it when she had no idea who the mermaid was that had taken it?

She neared a long strip of coral reef and spotted the claw of a familiar lobster.

"Carlos!" She swam faster to reach him before he could disappear into the coral.

"Shush! Shh!" Carlos waved his claw through the water.

"Carlos, please, I need to talk to you!" Bethany floated close to him.

"No! You need to get away before Kira finds me! We're playing hide and seek and she's it!"

"Oh!" Bethany frowned. "I'm sorry." She started to swim away, but as she turned, she slammed right into Kira.

"Oof!" Kira tumbled through the water while pointing at Carlos. "I found you!"

"No fair!" Carlos thrashed his claws through the water. "You never would have found me if Bethany hadn't given me away!"

"I'm sorry, I'm so sorry!" Bethany wiped at her eyes as fresh tears formed.

"Bethany?" Kira wrapped her arms around her. "What's wrong? Don't be upset. It's just a game. Carlos is just a sore loser."

"I didn't lose!" Carlos snapped his claws. "It wasn't a fair game!"

"Shush." Kira glared at him. "Can't you see that Bethany is upset?"

"Bethany?" Carlos swam over to her. "What's wrong, dear?"

As Bethany told them both what had happened, her voice trembled.

"Oh no! But how could a strange mermaid even know you had the gem?" Kira put her hands on her hips. "Something isn't right here."

"I know." Bethany shook her head. "But it doesn't matter. The gem is gone and it's all my fault."

"It's only the fault of the thief." Carlos shook his head. "You can't blame yourself for someone else doing something terrible."

"Maybe not, but I'm not sure that's how the queen will see it." Bethany frowned. "Avery went to check to see if her gem was still where she put it. Maybe you should check too, Kira."

"I will. Let's all meet up back here." She put her hand on Bethany's shoulder. "We're going to figure this out. Try not to worry."

Bethany nodded, but she still worried as Kira swam away.

Not long after Kira swam off, she saw Michelle swimming toward her. What would the princess of Eldoris have to say?

Soon Trina, Kira, and Avery joined her as well. As they all swam in her direction, Bethany got more and more nervous. Were their gems missing? Would they still want to help her?

"Bethany." Michelle paused in front of her. "I heard what happened. As soon as I did, I searched your room. I found something there." Michelle held up a strand of dark hair. "It was caught on the edge of your shell. With hair that long, I'll bet we could find more strands caught on things if we look around. Maybe we'll be able to figure out where she went."

"Maybe." Bethany nodded. She felt a little hopeful.

"We'll all help look." Trina swam forward. "None of our gems are missing. But that doesn't mean that this mermaid won't be back for them."

"And we have no idea what she might intend to do with the gem she stole." Avery crossed her arms.

"Carlos and I will start looking!" Bea, the sea slug, slithered off Trina's shoulder and floated off through the water. Carlos followed after her.

"Thank you so much for your help. I'm sorry that this happened." Bethany squeezed her hands together.

"It's not your fault." Michelle hugged her. "We need to find whoever did this and get your gem back. Then everything will be fine."

"I hope so." Bethany followed after the others as they began to spread out and look in all directions.

Maybe the hair was long, but the ocean was vast. Could they really find some kind of clue in such a big expanse? Bethany knew it was their only option, but she doubted that it would lead to much of anything.

As she searched through the coral for any evidence of the strange mermaid, she noticed a tiny seahorse tangled in some seaweed. "Are you okay, little fellow?" She reached down to tug at the seaweed.

"I can't get free," he whispered and wiggled a little. "I'm so tired from trying to get free."

"Let me see if I can help you." Bethany began to loosen the seaweed.

"Jasper! Jasper! Where are you?" a voice called out shrilly over the reef.

CHAPTER 4

Bethany looked up at the sound of the voice. She didn't recognize it, but she was too worried about the seahorse to pay attention to it. As she tugged the seaweed free, the seahorse swam up through the water.

"Ah that is so much better! Thank you!" He stretched his tail, then flipped over in the water. "It is so good to be free."

"How did you get tangled up in there in the first place?" Bethany looked at the seahorse quickly. "Don't you know better than to swim into seaweed?"

"I was trying to keep up with a friend of mine and I wasn't paying attention." He wiggled. "I won't make that mistake again!"

"Jasper!" The voice called out again. "Jasper, please, tell me where you are!"

"I'm here, Morgan! I'm here!" Jasper swam up through the water away from the coral. "I got stuck!"

"Oh, Jasper!" A mermaid swam toward him, a cloud of black hair billowing out behind her. "I thought I'd lost you forever!" She scooped the seahorse into her hands and drew him close to her. "I was so scared."

"You!" Bethany shrieked. She pointed her finger at the mermaid. "You stole my gem! I'm not letting you get away this time!"

"Oh no!" Morgan gulped, then bolted off in the other direction.

Bethany managed to grab a handful of her long hair before she could escape. She held onto it tightly.

"No you don't! Get back here! You're not going anywhere until you give me back my gem!"

"Let go of me!" Morgan growled. "You have no idea who you're dealing with!"

"Yes, I do!" Bethany wrapped her hand around the mermaid's hair. "A thief! That gem doesn't belong to you!"

Michelle, Avery, Kira, and Trina swam over quickly.

"Bethany, is this her?" Michelle glared at the other mermaid. "Is this the mermaid that stole your gem?"

"Yes it is!" Bethany smiled as her friends surrounded the other mermaid. "Now you'll never get away. You're going to have to answer to the queen."

"Oh, I'm so scared." Morgan rolled her eyes.

"You should be." Michelle swam closer to her. "My mother does not tolerate thieves."

"Your mother, huh?" Morgan smirked. "I guess that makes you a princess?"

"I guess it does." Michelle crossed her arms.

"I'm not scared of you either. I didn't do anything wrong." Morgan pursed her lips.

"How can you say that?" Bethany gasped. "You swam into my room and took my gem! It isn't yours! It doesn't belong to you! You stole it!"

"Well, you weren't using it, were you?" She scowled at Bethany. "None of you were. I thought you would be different. I thought you really cared about the humans."

"Cared about the humans?" Michelle raised an eyebrow. "What do you mean?"

"I mean, they need our help, and yet you won't do anything to help them." Morgan crossed her arms. "I've been following you and I thought that maybe you would do something great—maybe finally the mermaids of Eldoris would want to help the human world, but instead you all tucked away your gems and went back to your lives. None of you care what is happening to them."

"I don't understand what you mean." Bethany swam closer to her. "We're afraid of the humans. They could possibly destroy Eldoris. What do the humans have to be afraid of?"

"Are you kidding? They have no idea that they are destroying their own land, not to mention the rest of the planet." Morgan shook her head. "Don't you know anything about anything?"

"Planet?" Kira blinked.

"How are they destroying their land?" Trina frowned.

"Wow. I've heard that Eldoris mermaids don't know a lot, but I didn't think it was true." Morgan looked over at the seahorse. "Something tells me they haven't spent much time in the real ocean."

"What are you talking about?" Michelle shook her head. "This is the real ocean."

"Eldoris isn't the real ocean. It's not even close." Morgan crossed her arms. "The real ocean is full of trash, pollution, and danger. While you all float around your little paradise, the rest of the ocean is suffering and so is the human world. The only way to save it is to communicate with the humans, and you five are the only ones who have the ability to do that. But instead of using those gems to help the humans, you just hid them away and went on with your lives. How selfish is that?"

"Selfish?" Bethany frowned. "I never thought about it that way. It didn't seem safe to use the gems. Queen Maris said—"

"Queen Maris." Morgan sneered. "She wants everything to be safe. But the truth is, it's not safe. Not even Eldoris is safe. If we don't start working with the humans, no one and no place will ever be safe."

"She's just trying to scare us." Michelle pursed her lips. "We'll see what my mother has to say about all this. I'll go get some guards to bring her back to the Coral Palace."

She swam off.

"What do you mean no place will be safe?" Trina swam closer to Morgan.

"Do you really think we're all in danger?" Kira stared at her.

"I do." Morgan looked straight at Bethany. "If I didn't, I never would have stolen your gem. I don't believe it is ever right to steal. But sometimes things have to be done, even if they're not right. You can believe I'm a criminal or you can really listen to what I have to say and open your eyes to what is happening beyond Eldoris."

CHAPTER 5

"Don't listen to her." Avery swam a short distance away. "She's just trying to convince you to let her go. She's a thief and there's no explaining that."

"Please, you must listen to her." Jasper swam after Avery. "We've come all this way just for the chance to help the humans. We are not here to hurt you."

"Someone grab him!" Trina glared at the seahorse. "He's an accomplice."

"I'll get him!" Carlos leaped up from the sandy ocean floor with his claws clacking.

"No, wait!" Bethany scooped the seahorse up with her free hand. "Don't hurt him, please."

"Bethany?" Trina stared at her. "He probably helped her find your gem."

"Maybe he did, and maybe they're both wrong for what they did, but we don't know that for sure yet." She looked back at Morgan. "She risked a lot to get the gem and I have to believe it's because she really wanted to help."

"No, you don't have to believe that." Trina shook her head. "You could believe that she just wanted the gem for herself, so that she could trade it for something she wanted or maybe so that she could destroy it. She could be lying about all of this."

"Trina is right." Kira scooped Carlos up into her hands and helped him onto her shoulder. "We can't just take the word of a thief."

"Wait until Michelle gets back." Avery nodded. "She'll know what to do."

"If you turn me in to Queen Maris, you will never know the truth." Morgan looked around at each of them. "She may want to protect you, but that doesn't mean that she is telling you the truth. If none of you want to know, then I guess I was right to assume that you don't really care." She shrugged.

"I care." Bethany opened her hand so that Jasper could swim free. "I want to know the truth." She swam over to Morgan. "I've been dying to use the gem to communicate with humans. I don't know why we aren't allowed to."

"You're not allowed to because there is danger." Morgan smiled as Jasper swam up beside her cheek. But the smile faded as she looked back at Bethany. "Queen Maris isn't wrong to want to protect you. But the truth is, humans need protection too and so does the ocean that we share. If we don't start protecting them both, then it won't matter how safe Eldoris is."

"I don't understand." Bethany frowned.

"It would be easier if I showed you. But you'd have to trust me in order for me to do that." Morgan stared hard into Bethany's eyes. "Do you trust me?"

"Give me back my gem and I will let go of your hair." Bethany held out her free hand. "I want to trust you, but I can't let you have that."

"You weren't using it." Morgan's eyes flashed with anger. "Why should I give it back to you?"

"Because you can't use it either, Morgan. Only I can. I've

already tried it out. It's bonded to me and no one else. If you try to use it, it won't work."

"You tried it out?" Avery gasped. "When? Queen Maris told us not to."

"I know she did." Bethany frowned. "But I couldn't resist. I just wanted to see what it would be like. I put it on and I broke the surface. I just wanted to see if it would work."

"Did it?" Trina swam over, her eyes wide.

"Yes. But I only took a breath or two. I got scared and I took it off, promising myself that I'd never try it again." She looked back at Morgan. "But the gems are designed to work only for the people that they belong to. You wouldn't be able to use it, even if you tried."

"I know." Morgan shook her head. "I had heard that was the case. But I thought maybe it was still worth trying." She snapped her fingers and the gem appeared in the palm of her hand. "Bethany, I was only trying to do what I thought was the right thing. Really, I was."

"I know that." Bethany took the gem from Morgan's hand. "But it wasn't the right way to go about it."

She released Morgan's hair. "Please don't swim away. I want to know what you mean. I want to know how I can help."

"Bethany, this is a bad idea." Avery glared at Morgan. "We can't trust her."

"She gave me back the gem." Bethany looked over at the others. "I'm going with her. You don't have to, but I want to find out the truth. If the humans are in trouble—if the ocean is—if Eldoris is—then we need to find out why and how we can help. It's our job, remember?"

"Our job is to listen to the queen." Kira grabbed Bethany's hand. "We made her a promise, or don't you remember?"

"I do remember. But she can't always know what's best. She's just a mermaid, like the rest of us. She can make mistakes too and this might be a mistake she's making." Bethany closed her eyes for a moment, then opened them again. "I have to believe that if Eldoris is really in danger, she would want us to do whatever we could to protect it."

"Bethany's right." Trina swam over to her. "It can't hurt to find out more about the humans and how they might need our help. I'm going with her."

"Michelle will be back very soon with the guards." Avery glanced nervously over her shoulder. "If we're going to go, we need to go right now."

"You too?" Kira shook her head. "You're all going to believe this stranger over our queen?"

"It's not that I don't believe Queen Maris." Avery looked back at Kira. "I just know that she wouldn't do anything that would put us in danger. She wants to protect us all so badly. But sometimes we have to take risks. Sometimes there has to be a little danger in order for us to protect everyone who needs it. Kira, you don't have to come."

"I'm going. If all of you are going, I'm going too." Kira narrowed her eyes. "But just remember that I told you that we can't trust her. She's not from Eldoris and she's a thief."

CHAPTER 6

"Believe what you want." Morgan flicked her tail through the water. "Just try your best to keep up."

She took off through the water.

Bethany tried to swim as fast as Morgan did. She stroked her arms swiftly through the water. She flailed her tail as fast as she could, but still Morgan remained far ahead of her.

A quick glance over Bethany's shoulder revealed that the other mermaids were quite a distance behind her. She swam faster than them, but she still couldn't catch up to Morgan.

"Morgan! Wait! You're going to leave us behind!" Bethany's heart raced, both from swimming so fast and from fear, as she realized she had no idea what part of the ocean they were in anymore. She couldn't figure out how to get back to Eldoris. What if Morgan swam off and left them lost in the middle of the ocean?

"What is it?" Morgan swam back toward her.

"We can't keep up, you're going to leave us behind." Bethany frowned. "I thought you said I could trust you?"

"I thought I told you to keep up." Morgan smirked.

"How did you learn to swim so fast?" Bethany floated in the water, grateful for the chance to rest.

"When you live outside the walls of Eldoris, you have to swim fast. There are many dangers to escape."

"Why do you live outside of Eldoris?" Bethany swam up beside her. "Wouldn't you rather be safe?"

"My parents wanted to do things differently. They wanted to embrace the humans and even risk being discovered by them. They didn't agree with hiding away and keeping our worlds separate." She shrugged. "I didn't know any different, I was too small. And now I'm alone."

"What happened to your parents?" Bethany stared at her. "Why are you alone now?"

"They were swept away in a terrible storm. I have no idea where they ended up. I lost contact with the other mermaids in my tribe." She bit into her bottom lip. "All I have now is Jasper."

"I'm so sorry." Bethany frowned. "I would hate to be alone."

"It's not so bad really. You get used to it." She swam faster and left Bethany behind.

Bethany hung back until the others caught up with her.

"We need to make sure she's okay. She has no one else to protect her." Bethany shook her head. "No wonder she's so reckless. She doesn't think she has anything to lose."

"Well, we do." Kira narrowed her eyes. "We need to make sure she doesn't swim us right into the middle of a disaster zone."

Ahead of them, Morgan floated in the water, no longer swimming. The water appeared murkier and thicker in some way.

"Here it is." Morgan spoke up as the others gathered around her. "You can barely see through the water here."

"What is this place?" Bethany started to swim forward for a closer look.

"Don't!" Morgan placed her hand on Bethany's shoulder to stop her. "It's a dumping ground for toxic stuff." She looked over at Bethany. "The humans pour it in here, because they don't know what else to do with it. They ignore the fact that it kills sea life and pollutes the ocean."

"This is terrible." Trina swam forward, but not past Morgan. "How could they be so stupid?"

"Because they have no one to teach them." Bethany frowned. "That's why we need to help them. They don't even understand what they are doing. How can they, when they don't live in the ocean? They can't see the results of their actions."

"I would think that anyone would know that it was foolish to put stuff like this in the water." Kira narrowed her eyes.

"They don't know how to get rid of the sludge they create. But with our help, we can come up with solutions that won't harm the ocean or their land. We can make our entire planet a better place for all of us." Morgan turned to face them. "But only if we're willing to take the risk of communicating with them."

"What if they don't want to communicate with us?" Trina raised an eyebrow. "It's not like they are going to welcome us with open arms. We are monsters to them."

"Monsters? How could we be monsters?" Kira glanced at Carlos. "Do you really think that's how they see us?"

"Some will." Morgan nodded. "But others will be happy to work with us. We just have to find the right ones."

"How will we know who the right ones are?" Bethany looked over at Morgan. "What if we pick the wrong ones and we don't know it until it's too late?"

"That's the risk." Morgan crossed her arms. "There's no way to be sure. I'm willing to take that risk, but as soon as I break the surface, I can't breathe. There's nothing I can do to communicate with them. You, on the other hand..." She looked straight into Bethany's eyes. "You have a way to speak their language, to breathe their air, to blend our worlds so that we can save them. How can you just pretend that you don't? Isn't that about the same as dumping toxic sludge into the ocean?"

"Not even close." Kira crossed her arms.

"She's not wrong," Bethany whispered. "If we know this is happening and there's a way we can stop it, but we don't, then we're being just as stupid as the humans who do this."

"Bethany, there's a lot more to it than that." Avery swam up beside her. "We've always been taught to protect Eldoris, to never let humans know we exist. There are reasons for that."

"There are." Bethany nodded. "But maybe those reasons aren't more important than the good of our ocean and of the land that the humans live on. If we need each other in order to live in harmony, then refusing to communicate only hurts us all."

"I don't know." Trina huffed. "It all seems pretty risky to me."

Bethany stared at Trina. She knew her friend to be very brave. If the idea of speaking to humans scared Trina, then she knew it should scare her as well. For some reason, that fear wasn't enough to stop her curiosity.

CHAPTER 7

"I did spot a particular group of humans. Three of them. They seem pretty interested in our ocean and helping it. But they are young." Morgan tipped her head to the side. "My plan was to try to speak to them, to make it clear that if they are willing to help, then we will help too. But obviously, that can't happen now." She looked at Bethany. "Unless you're willing to try."

"Show me the three humans you think might help. I'll decide then." Bethany felt mesmerized by the confidence and urgency in Morgan's voice. Perhaps it was the mystery that surrounded the other mermaid or maybe just the way that she shared her passion, but Bethany felt drawn to her.

"Bethany, this is probably a bad idea." Kira frowned.

"I'm going." Bethany turned to face her friends. "Look, I know what I'm asking is a lot. We are not following the queen's rules and we are taking risks that we probably shouldn't. I want you all to know that you don't have to join me. Morgan and I can go alone."

"And leave you alone with her?" Trina crossed her arms. "Not a chance."

"We're with you, Bethany." Bea stuck her head up in the water. "We all have to do what we can to protect our ocean."

"I'm just curious, does this trio of humans happen to eat lobster?" Carlos hid in Kira's hair.

"I can't promise you that these humans aren't dangerous." Morgan looked off through the murky water. "But at this point, I think they're our only chance. Follow me." She swam through the water, slow enough for the others to keep up.

Bethany began to feel tired as they continued to swim for what felt like hours. By the time the water became shallow, she didn't want to swim another inch.

"Where are we?" She floated beside Morgan when she finally stopped swimming. "We have to be so far away from Eldoris."

"Actually, we're not too far from it. I had to take us the long way here, because all around this area are fishing boats with large nets. We can't risk getting caught in them. They're very difficult to get free from." She pointed ahead of her. "There is a small inlet up here—a cove—where I've seen the three humans spend a lot of time. I've watched them for a while. They are always cleaning up the water and caring for the creatures that live in it."

"So, we're supposed to overlook the fishing boats with nets and believe these three humans are somehow different?" Trina swam toward the shallow water. "What if we break the surface and the humans decide to alert those in the boats?"

"Trina is right." Avery frowned. "It makes me nervous to think that boats are so close by."

"What makes you think these three humans are different?" Bethany turned her attention back to Morgan. "You said you've been watching them. What makes you trust them?"

"They're young, like us. I think their minds are still wide open. Queen Maris has rules, but you chose not to follow them because you thought it was best. You're a free-thinker. These girls seem the same way to me. They are willing to do things differently, because they think it's right. Just see for yourself." She held her hand out to Bethany. "I'll show you where they spend most of their time."

"Alright." She took Morgan's hand.

"We'll be right behind you." Trina swam up beside Bethany.

"No." Bethany looked back at them. "The water is so shallow and pretty clear. If we all go, they're sure to notice us. Let me take a look at them first. Then I'll let you know what I see."

"Are you sure?" Avery eyed Morgan suspiciously.

"I'm sure." Bethany smiled. "I'll be fine. I have the gem, remember?"

"Be careful." Kira met her eyes.

"I will be." Bethany turned as Morgan gave her hand a light tug.

"Sometimes I send Jasper out to greet them." Morgan pointed toward the rocks that jutted out into the water. "They love to see him. Do you want to go say hi, Jasper?" She looked at the seahorse.

"Sure." Jasper swam ahead of them. Moments later squeals could be heard from above the water.

"What's that sound?" Bethany shivered.

"Don't worry. It's a happy sound. It sounds different when it comes through the water, but it just means they're excited." Morgan guided her behind a large rock. "Sometimes I peek around this at them." She began to lift her head toward the surface.

"Wait. Are you sure it's safe?" Bethany started to pull her back down.

"I'm not sure, but I'm willing to find out. Are you?" Morgan locked her eyes to Bethany's, then began to swim to the surface again.

Bethany's heart pounded as she watched Morgan break through the surface. A second later, she followed after her. When she felt the air on her face, she knew there was no turning back. Morgan pointed around the rock at three human girls that stood near the edge of the water. All seemed to be quite excited by the seahorse.

"I can't believe he came back to see us." A dark-haired girl grinned.

"It's because we keep this cove so clean." A blonde girl smiled.

"It's because I'm his favorite." A red-haired girl laughed as she began to climb across the rocks that lined the cove.

"Be careful, Jessie, those rocks are slippery!" The dark-haired girl put her hands on her hips.

"Relax, I've walked across them so many times. I'll be fine." Jessie continued to walk further out on the rocks.

"Rachel is right, Jessie, the currents are so strong in the water. If you fall in, you'll be out to sea before you know it." The blonde-haired girl stared after her. "You should be more careful."

"I'm fine, Val!" Jessie swung her hands through the air as she stepped onto another rock. "I see a piece of plastic out at the end. I just want to grab it before it can get caught on any sea turtles!" Jessie continued out across the rocks.

CHAPTER 8

Bethany sank back down under the water. She couldn't help but be amused by the way the girls talked to one another. It reminded her of the way she and her own friends talked to one another.

"What did you see?" Avery swam up beside her.

"I thought I told you to wait back there?" Bethany frowned as she looked from Avery to Kira and Trina, who swam up behind her.

"We couldn't let you be out here without us." Avery frowned. "We have to keep an eye on each other. That's what friends do."

"Yes, I guess it is." Bethany smiled. "The three girls that Morgan found look like they might really listen to us if we tried to talk to them. What could it hurt to just try?'

"It could expose us all, that's how it could hurt." Trina watched as Morgan sank back down under the water. "How can you be sure that these girls won't scream and run in the other direction?"

"I've watched them gently lead a school of fish out of the cove. I've watched them draw pictures in the sand of sea creatures, both real and imagined. They love the sea and the creatures that live in it." Morgan looked at the other mermaids. "I know that none of you have any reason to believe me, but I think these humans can help us if we just give them the chance."

A splash in the water drew all their attention. As they watched, Jessie sank down into the water with a piece of plastic clutched in her hand.

"Watch out! She'll see us!" Avery swam toward the rock that Morgan had hidden behind.

"Can't she swim?" Bethany stared at the little girl as she sank further and further down into the water.

"Yes, she can swim. They all can." Morgan stared as well. "I don't know why she isn't."

"She's hurt." Kira peered through the water. "She must have hit her head on the rocks when she fell. There's a bit of blood around her."

"Oh no!" Bethany's eyes widened. "That's why she's not moving. She's knocked out."

"I'm sure her friends will jump in to help her." Trina looked up toward the surface of the water. "Any second now they'll be jumping in."

"Not if they didn't see her fall." Bethany gulped as she looked up at the surface as well. "Not if they're too busy watching Jasper swim around. They probably didn't see her slip." She looked back at Jessie. "She's almost at the bottom! Even if she wakes up now, she probably won't make it to the surface."

"Bethany, we have to stay out of this." Trina put her hand on Bethany's shoulder. "There's no way we can save her without being seen."

"We have to save her. We can't let her drown." Bethany swam forward.

"Wait!" Avery frowned. "If we try to save her, we're going to be exposed. There's no way to get around it. Humans will see us. They'll know once and for all that mermaids exist."

"Even if they do, I'll risk it. I can't let her die, Avery! She's the same age as us! What if it were me? Would you just sit by and watch?" Bethany shook her head. "You don't have to answer that, because I know that you wouldn't."

She pulled away from her friend and swam straight toward Jessie. Already she could see that the little girl was taking in water. She knew that humans couldn't breathe under water. They had to hold their breath, just like she had to when she broke the surface of the water.

She realized, as she neared Jessie's limp body, that she was going to need to breathe outside of the water if she hoped to save the girl. She snapped her fingers and her gem appeared in the palm of her hand. She pressed the gem against her neck and felt it begin to bond with her skin.

Immediately her chest began to tighten. She held her breath, aware that she could no longer breathe under water. She wrapped her arms around the girl and began to swim up to the surface.

As her chest grew tighter and tighter, her eyes began to burn. She needed to breathe so badly and Jessie felt heavy in her arms. She flicked her tail as hard as she could, but the surface still seemed too far away.

Just as she began to panic, she felt arms around her. Her friends, including Morgan, pushed her upward toward the surface of the water. The final shove was enough to allow her to break through the surface of the water.

Her lips spread wide open and she took a deep breath of the air for the very first time. The air felt fresh and smoother than she'd expected. It filled her lungs and made her feel connected with the sky that stretched out above her.

"Jessie!" Panicked shouts echoed all around her. "Jessie!"

Bethany realized that Jessie's friends had figured out that she'd gone missing and they were searching for her. Bethany swam toward the edge of the water. She floated Jessie in front of her, with her head above the water. Her eyes were closed and Bethany could tell from the stillness of Jessie's body that she wasn't breathing.

"Here she is, over here!" she called out. Her voice sounded strange to her own ears. It was sharper than she expected, as if speaking outside of the water made her words harsher. Some of her words jumbled up as well, as she wasn't used to breathing around her words.

"Jessie!" Val shrieked. "Rachel! She's over here!"

Bethany shuddered as the two girls splashed into the water and headed straight for her. The sight of humans looking at her —running toward her—inspired great fear within her. She had to resist the urge to toss Jessie into the water and swim off. Some things were more important than being safe.

Jessie needed her help and she wasn't going to turn back now.

CHAPTER 9

As Bethany reached the rocks along the edge of the water, the two other human girls gathered close.

"Is she okay?" Val asked.

"What happened to her head?" Rachel frowned when she saw the wound on Jessie's head.

"I think she must have slipped on the rocks." Bethany looked between the two of them. "We need to get her flat on the ground. She has swallowed a lot of water."

"Oh no, oh no!" Val clasped her hands together. Then she reached for Jessie's arm. "Let's go, Rachel, we need to help!"

"I've got her legs." Rachel tried to grab Jessie's legs, but they slipped out of her grasp.

Bethany lunged forward and began to shimmy up on the rocks with Jessie in her arms. By the time she got Jessie onto the beach, Bethany was fully out of the water. Her tail flicked against the rocks as she leaned over Jessie.

"You're a—" Rachel stumbled backwards.

"How can you be?" Val sank down into the sand.

Bethany focused on Jessie. She breathed into her mouth,

then tipped her body to the side. "We have to get the water out of her, we can't wait any longer."

"I know what to do." Rachel jumped up. She began to push on Jessie's chest.

Seconds later, Jessie coughed up some water, then opened her eyes.

"Oh, my head hurts." She frowned as she pressed her fingers against the bump on her head.

"I told you those rocks were slippery!" Val huffed, then threw her arms around her friend. "I'm so glad that you're okay."

"Am I?" Jessie stared at Bethany—or more specifically at Bethany's very long tail. "Maybe I hit my head way too hard. I think I might need to go to the hospital." She blinked.

"It's okay." Bethany shivered as she felt their eyes on her. "I won't hurt you." She knew that she wouldn't. But she wasn't so sure that they wouldn't hurt her.

"Are you a mermaid?" Rachel's eyes widened. "I mean, is that even possible?"

"It is." Bethany ran her hand down along her tail. "I am a mermaid."

"But you're not real." Val crossed her arms. "We know you're not. We've studied every kind of sea creature, and mermaids are definitely not real."

"I am very real." Bethany smiled. "There was a time that I didn't think humans were real. It's safer for us to let humans believe we don't exist."

"You look young." Jessie peered at her. "Like us."

"I am." She frowned as she glanced back at the water. "I can't stay long. I have a special gem." She touched the gem on her neck as she looked back at them. "It lets me breathe outside the water, but I can't use it for too long."

"You used it so that you could save me, didn't you?" Jessie looked into her eyes. "I almost drowned, didn't I?"

"I wanted to make sure that you were safe." Bethany nodded. "But that isn't the only reason I came out of the water." She looked from one shocked face to the next. "We need your help."

"We?" Val whispered. "You mean there are more of you?"

"I have to take a picture!" Rachel reached into her pocket.

"No, don't!" Jessie gasped and jumped in front of Bethany. "We need to protect her, don't you see, Rachel? If other people find out about her and the other mermaids, then they'll be in danger."

"She's right." Bethany frowned. "Many humans would want to harm us. That's why we have always hidden from humans."

"Until today." Jessie turned back to face her.

"Until today." Bethany took a deep breath of the fresh air. "We thought that maybe you and your friends would be willing to help us. You seem to care so much for the water. My friend Morgan has been watching you for some time. She trusted that you would help us, and I trusted her. I hope that we weren't wrong to offer that trust."

"You weren't wrong." Jessie smiled. "I promise. We would be happy to help you in any way that we can."

"Maybe if humans and mermaids can find a way to work together, we can help each other to protect the land and the sea." Bethany held out her hand. "My name is Bethany."

"Bethany." Jessie smiled as she shook her hand. "I'm Jessie and this is Val and Rachel."

"It's nice to meet all of you." Bethany touched the gem on her neck. "I think I need to go back now. But maybe we could meet here again sometime?"

"Absolutely!" Jessie clapped her hands. "We will be here!"

"I will be back soon." Bethany smiled at the three of them. "Jessie, please be careful on the rocks."

"I will!" Jessie waved to her as Bethany slid back into the water.

Her heart filled with warmth as she pulled the gem free from her neck. Morgan had been right. The girls wanted to help and they were kind creatures.

"Bethany!" Morgan shouted through the water and waved her hand. "Hurry! We are in grave danger!"

"What do you mean?" Bethany frowned. "Everything went well with the girls."

"It's not that." Morgan grabbed her hand and pointed to the other mermaids, who were swimming ahead of them. "The fishing boats are coming close. They are going to trap us in the cove if we don't get out of here soon. When the tide goes out, the water won't be deep enough for us to breathe. We have to hurry!"

"Oh no!" Bethany swam after her as fear flooded through her.

CHAPTER 10

Everywhere they turned, large fishing nets hovered. The shadows of boats above them haunted them.

"What are we going to do?" Bethany swam close to Avery and Trina. "Can we get past them?"

"We're going to have to try." Trina frowned. "It's the only way we're going to get out of here."

"But we have to be very careful. If we get tangled, we might not be able to get free." Kira shivered.

"Don't worry." Carlos scuttered along below, close to Kira. "I would get you free, I promise."

"Thank you, Carlos." She patted the top of his head. "But I'm hoping you won't have to do that."

"Let's go that way." Morgan pointed to a gap between two big fishing nets. "If we can get through there, we'll be safe. But we have to be quick."

"That's easy for you to say." Trina shot Morgan a sharp look. "You're faster than any creature in the sea. But the rest of us aren't that fast."

"That's why you'll go in front of me." Morgan locked her eyes to Trina's. "I meant what I said. I don't want to cause any harm. We may be different, Trina, but I still want you to be safe."

"We don't have time to argue." Avery gave them both a push. "We have to get through before the gap closes."

"She's right." Bethany began to swim forward. "Let's go, we have to hurry." She grabbed Avery's hand. "Let's stay together. Everyone hold on so no one gets left behind."

As the mermaids formed a chain, Morgan was the last link. Trina led them forward through the gap in the fishing nets. Once she was through, she looked back over her shoulder.

"Let's go, Avery!" She gave her hand a tug to pull her through.

"Kira!" Avery tugged on Kira's hand just as the nets began to slide closer together.

"Hurry!" Kira cried out and pulled hard on Bethany's hand.

"Morgan!" Bethany gasped and swam forward as quickly as she could, while still clinging to Morgan's hand.

"Just keep going!" Morgan shouted. "Don't stop! Just keep going!"

Bethany felt the rough rope of one of the nets brush against her arm. She winced as it scraped her skin. It bulged with fish and other creatures trapped inside of it. Her heart hurt as she wished that she could set them all free. She had to focus instead on getting through the nets so that Morgan could make it through too.

"Hurry!" Avery cried out.

"We're almost there." Bethany forced herself to look forward. She had no choice but to just keep swimming forward. As they neared the end of the gap, she turned back to look at Morgan. "Let's go! Swim, Morgan!"

"I can't!" Morgan wriggled, but she didn't move forward. "My tail is caught in one of the nets. Just go, Bethany! Get through to the other side!"

"No!" Bethany let go of Avery's hand but not Morgan's. She reached back and ran her hand along Morgan's tail until she found the net. Then she pried Morgan's tail free from it.

"Now, Morgan! Swim!"

Morgan wrapped her arm around Bethany's waist and together they both swam through the tiny sliver of space left between the two huge nets. Once on the other side, Morgan released her.

"We did it!" Bethany grinned.

"You shouldn't have come back for me!" Morgan stared at her. "You took too big a risk."

"Some things are worth taking a risk for." Bethany met her eyes. "Friendship is one of them."

"Thank you." Morgan hugged her and held her tight. "You're a great friend."

A horrible shriek carried through the water. At the sound of it, Bethany pulled away from Morgan. She spun around to face the nets.

"What was that?" She heard the shriek again. Then Bethany noticed a flash of a familiar tail through the many fish that cluttered one of the nets. Her heart skipped a beat. It wasn't possible, was it? As far as she knew Michelle was still back at the Coral Palace.

"Michelle?" She swam toward the net.

"Get back here, Bethany!" Trina shouted at her. "Don't get so close!"

The shriek carried through the water again and Bethany felt bumps rise up on her arms. It wasn't just a shriek. It was a cry for help. She saw the tail thrash and then Michelle's face pressed up against the net.

"Oh no!" Bethany cried out. "It can't be!"

"Bethany!" Avery pleaded. "Come over here! You're going to get swept up in the net!"

"That's Michelle!" Bethany gasped as she pointed to the mermaid caught in the net. "She can't get free! We have to save her!"

"Michelle?" Kira swam forward. "Are you sure? But she shouldn't be here!"

"She must have come looking for us!" Bethany swam toward the net. "We have to get her out!" She reached for the ropes, but before she could grasp them, the net began to slide through the water. "No, wait!" She gasped and tried to catch up with it. "Michelle!"

Morgan swam up beside her, then bolted past her. "I'll get her, Bethany! I'll get her!" She swam so fast that she left waves in her wake.

Bethany tried to swim just as fast, but it wasn't long before she was too tired to keep up.

"Michelle!" she cried out again. In the distance, she saw the net with Michelle still trapped inside and Morgan swimming after her.

"Bethany!" Avery swam up to her with Trina and Kira at her side. "We're going to get her back, Bethany. Don't be afraid, we're going to get her back!"

BOOK 6: MORGAN

CHAPTER 1

Morgan swam as fast as she could after Eldoris's Princess Michelle, who had been captured in a fishing net. She knew that if she didn't save the mermaid two things would happen. The entire mermaid community would face a tragic loss and the entire mermaid community would face a great danger.

Once the fishermen discovered what was hidden in their net, mermaids would be exposed once and for all—not to humans they could hopefully trust, but to people that might see Michelle as a monster.

Even though Morgan was one of the fastest swimmers in the sea, she was no match for the boat that chugged along through the water at an effortless speed. Her arms began to ache and her tail grew too weak to propel her forward.

As she began to drift through the water she started to panic.

Was this all her fault? She had encouraged the other mermaids to journey with her to meet the humans, and if she hadn't, Michelle would most likely not have ended up in that net.

As she sank down toward the bottom of the ocean, her body felt heavy—not just from being tired, but from a great sadness that filled her. She had promised the others that she would save Michelle, but she hadn't been able to keep that promise. Now Eldoris would never welcome her or forgive her. As she began to cry, a soft voice called out to her.

"Morgan, I'm here, my friend." Jasper swam up beside her ear. "You did your best. You just couldn't catch that boat."

"It's going to go to shore." She looked up at the seahorse. "Once it does, there will be no way any of us can save her. None of us can go on land."

"That may be true, but it doesn't mean we can't save her still." Jasper looked into her eyes. "Remember, we made some friends that do have legs—that can go on land."

"The human girls?" Morgan's eyes widened. "You're right, they are land creatures. They might be able to help us."

"And after Bethany saved one of them, I'm sure they would be happy to help." Jasper looked back through the water. "But we are a long way from their cove and you need to rest before you can swim again."

"I need to get back to them." Morgan began to float up into the water, but her tail ached so badly that it wouldn't offer one flip.

"Rest now." Jasper swam around her. "You can't help anyone when you're this worn out. Once you can swim again, we can go back to the others."

"No, we can't." Morgan sighed as she closed her eyes. "The other mermaids will never trust me again. They have no reason to. I caused all this by leading them into a place I never should have."

"You couldn't have known that Michelle would come looking for them. You couldn't have known that she would be caught in one of the fishing nets." Jasper settled in the crook of her elbow. "It's important to remember just how brave you are. You didn't steal that gem to hurt anyone, you stole it to help save all the mermaids and all the humans. You did something good. Yes, something terrible happened, but it wasn't your fault."

"I hope that one day I can believe that." Morgan frowned. "But even if I can, I don't think the other mermaids ever will." She felt her body begin to relax as she drifted off to sleep. She could no longer stay awake. She'd used up every ounce of energy that existed within her and yet she'd failed to save Michelle. Her stomach twisted into knots as she thought of how the other mermaids would react when they found out.

Hours later, she felt the water around her rock. It rocked so hard that her eyes opened instantly. Only a creature of great size could disrupt the water that much—which meant that a very large predator was likely on its way.

"Jasper!" She caught him in her hand as she swam up through the water. "We have to swim fast!"

"Wait!" Jasper clung to her fingertip as she began to swim. "Morgan, please wait!"

"There's no time!" She glanced over her shoulder and saw a giant shadow draw closer to her. "Hide, Jasper! Hide!" She shrieked as the shadow drew closer and closer.

Usually, she sensed danger long before it reached her, but the deep sleep she'd been in must have prevented her from sensing what had approached. The murky water made it difficult for her to make out just what it was.

A great white shark? A killer whale? A mammoth deep-sea creature that had come up to more shallow water to feed? She'd seen many terrifying things as she lived outside of the protection of Eldoris.

As her heart pounded, she had the feeling that whatever was about to consume her was far worse than anything she'd ever seen.

"Morgan?" a voice called out to her. It wasn't Jasper. It was too far away for her to make out who it belonged to. Could the creature somehow know her name?

"Help!" Morgan cried out, hoping that perhaps the voice belonged to someone who could rescue her. "Please help me!"

"Morgan!" the voice cried out again and the shadow drew closer.

Morgan began to make out just how large it was. Far larger than her, which meant it probably had quite a large mouth too.

"Oh no!" She covered her face and balled herself up as much as she could. "Please don't eat me, I promise I don't taste very good!"

The water around her rippled. She braced herself and waited for giant jaws to close around her.

Instead, she heard something that sounded quite a bit like laughter.

CHAPTER 2

"No one is going to eat you, Morgan." Avery peered down at her from the shell of a very large sea turtle. "I called my friend to help us catch up to you. Morgan, this is Tommy. Tommy, this is Morgan. Trust me, Tommy doesn't eat mermaids."

"Not even when I'm very hungry." Tommy grinned. "Although I have been known to nibble."

"Really?" Morgan peeked out from behind her hands. She looked at the giant turtle with wide eyes. "I'd rather you didn't nibble at all."

"I can respect that." He bowed his head in the water.

"Where's Michelle?" Bethany peered past Morgan. "Is she hurt?"

"Uh." Morgan looked down at her hands as they hovered in the water in front of her. "I tried to keep up, but I just couldn't."

"What do you mean you couldn't?" Trina swam down from the back of the turtle. "You swim faster than any creature I've ever seen."

"Any creature, yes." She frowned. "But not faster than any boat. I'm so sorry. I swam after it for as long as I could, but I had to rest."

"Oh no!" Kira floated down beside them. "You mean she's gone? She's really gone?"

"I'm so sorry." Morgan looked at each mermaid in turn. "I never meant for any of this to happen. I know you probably don't believe me."

"I believe you." Kira held out her hand to Morgan. "I know you tried as hard as you could."

"Thank you." Morgan took her hand, then looked at the others. "Michelle is gone and I can't tell you exactly where she went, but I think there might be a way we can still find her and save her."

"How?" Trina frowned. "She's already been gone for hours."

"We're far from land. The boat probably hasn't made it back yet. There's a good chance that Michelle hasn't been discovered. But we're not going to be able to do it without help." She glanced at Jasper.

"We should go back and tell Queen Maris." Bethany crossed her arms. "She could send out all the guards to help."

"No!" Morgan shook her head. "We can't tell her. She will find out about everything we did, including contacting the humans."

"It's her daughter." Bethany stared at her. "She needs to know that Michelle has been taken."

"There's no time." Trina swam between the two of them. "Yes, the queen should know, but if we take the time to go back to tell her, all we'll be able to say is that Michelle is gone forever. If we stay here and try to save her, then maybe we will be able to return with better news."

"Then let's stop talking about it and start getting this rescue mission underway." Kira looked at the other mermaids. "We have to get back to the cove and hope that the human girls come back. It's the only way we're going to get any help with finding the fishing boat."

"Tommy can take us." Avery swam over to the turtle. "But he won't be as fast as Morgan."

"I can get there fast." Morgan nodded. "But I won't be able to communicate with the humans."

"I'll swim with you." Bethany met her eyes. "That way I can talk with them."

"You won't be able to keep up." Morgan frowned. "I swim very fast."

"Then I'll hold on." Bethany grabbed Morgan's hand and smiled. "I'll do my best to keep up, and if not, you can pull me along."

"I've never done that before." Morgan quirked an eyebrow. "But I guess I could try."

"We have to do something." Bethany nodded. "And fast. There's no time to waste. If we're going to get the human girls to help, we've got to get there as fast as we can."

"Let's do it." Morgan squeezed Bethany's hand. "We'll meet the rest of you there." Morgan looked intently at them. "Be careful."

"We will be." Kira nodded. "Michelle wouldn't want any of us getting hurt, not even to save her."

Morgan began to swim with Bethany's hand still clasped in hers. It took a bit of adjustment for her to get used to swimming with a partner, but soon their arms and tails were moving at the exact same time. She couldn't swim quite as fast as usual, but it was still faster than what Bethany was used to.

"Wow, everything looks so different when you're moving this fast." Bethany tightened her grasp on Morgan's hand. "It's beautiful."

"Blurry." Morgan laughed, then continued to focus on swimming.

As the water began to get warmer, she knew that they were getting close to the shallow part of the cove. Her heart began to pound, both from exhaustion and from fear. Would the humans be there to help them? Would they be willing to help?

She had promised the others that connecting with the humans would be a good thing, but she couldn't know that for sure. After seeing Bethany, the three human girls might have gone home and told everyone what they'd seen. They might be about to arrive at the cove to discover that it was full of humans that wanted to catch them the same way that Michelle had been caught.

A ripple of panic carried through Morgan and she began to slow.

"What's wrong?" Bethany glanced over at her. "Are you tired?"

"We should let Jasper go ahead of us and check things out." Morgan looked at the seahorse. "Can you make sure it's safe?"

"Of course I will. Be back in a snap!" He smiled, then wiggled off through the water.

"Do you think the girls might have told others about me?" Bethany frowned. "Do you think they might have set a trap?"

"I hope they didn't, but we need to be careful. The only way we can save Michelle is if we don't get caught ourselves." She watched as Jasper swam toward the shallow water. "We'll know whether we can trust the humans soon enough."

CHAPTER 3

Morgan bit into her bottom lip as she waited for the seahorse to return. She wanted to think positive, but in her experience, whatever could go wrong, did go wrong. She'd spent a lot of time hiding in coral or behind piles of rocks because a predator had spotted her.

The humans were no different. They were still predators. They were just dangerous in a different way.

"Where is he?" Bethany squinted through the water. "Maybe we should get a little closer?"

"A little." Morgan nodded as she swam forward. "He'll be back soon."

"He seems like a good friend." Bethany swam forward as well. "You're lucky to have him."

"Yes, I am." Morgan smiled. "We've been friends for a long time."

"What is it like?" Bethany looked over at her. "Living in the beyond?"

"It's an adventure." Morgan laughed. Then her smile faded as she looked at Bethany. "Actually, to be honest, it's pretty lonely. I got separated from the rest of the mermaids a long time ago, and since then, it's just been me and Jasper."

"Well, it's not just the two of you anymore." Bethany wrapped her arm around her shoulders. "You have all of us now."

"Even after what happened to Michelle?" Morgan met her eyes.

"It wasn't your fault, Morgan. And the important thing is that you are helping us to get her back." Bethany looked up at a small splash in the water. "Here comes Jasper."

"What did you find, Jasper?" Morgan swam up to meet him.

"Nothing." He wiggled closer to Morgan. "There is no sign of any human at the cove. But the sun isn't quite up yet. It's possible that they're still coming."

"Oh no." Morgan frowned. "We have no choice but to wait."

"Wait?" Avery slid off Tommy's shell as she and the rest of the mermaids arrived. "Wait for what?"

"The humans aren't there yet." Bethany frowned. "Without their help, there's no way we can save Michelle. We have to wait for them."

"What if they don't come?" Kira swam back and forth, her eyes wide. "What if this is the day that they decide they don't want to visit the cove? What if it rains?"

"They come even in the rain." Morgan lifted her head out of the water far enough to see the land, then ducked back down under. "Trust me, they'll be here."

"Trust you?" Trina glared at her. "Isn't that what we did in the first place?"

"This isn't the time to start fighting." Kira held up her hands. "If we have any hope of getting Michelle back, it's going to be because we worked together, not because we fought with one another."

"Kira is right." Bethany floated close to Morgan. "Without

Morgan or the humans, we'd have no chance of saving Michelle. We need to stay positive. We will rescue Michelle. We have to."

"I'm trying." Trina frowned. "I'm sorry, Morgan."

"It's alright." Morgan patted her shoulder. "I can see how much you all care about Michelle. She's very lucky to have all of you to worry about her."

"Maybe I can help!" Carlos untangled himself from Kira's hair and settled to the sea bottom just under them. "I can go up on the shore and watch for the girls. Maybe I can get them to come here faster."

"Are you sure you want to do that, Carlos?" Kira frowned. "It's a risk to you too, you know."

"Don't worry about me!" Carlos snapped his claws. "I know how to handle the humans. I'll have them here in a flash!" He scuttled toward the shore.

Kira swam after him until the water got too shallow for her. The other mermaids gathered close.

Moments later Morgan heard a strange sound. It was something between a squeal and a shriek.

"What is that?" She narrowed her eyes.

"I'm not sure." Bethany blinked.

"It sounds awful." Avery covered her ears.

Morgan poked her head above the water, just far enough to see the shore. She spotted Carlos with his claws waving through the air and the three human girls running away from him. She sank back down under the water.

"I think we have a problem." She cringed. "Carlos is scaring off our human friends."

"They're scared of a lobster?" Kira rolled her eyes. "How silly."

"Oh really?" Trina laughed. "I can recall someone who was pretty scared when she first met Carlos."

"Well, that was a long time ago!" Kira huffed.

"I'll see if I can get their attention." Bethany frowned as she placed the gem against her neck. "We don't have time for them to make friends with Carlos."

"Be careful. We can't be sure that they will be friendly." Trina met her eyes. "First sign of trouble, you get back under the water. Got it?"

"Got it." Bethany nodded.

"And keep an eye on how you feel." Avery swam close to her. "We have no idea how long the gem will last before you won't be able to breathe under water anymore."

"I'll be careful." Bethany smiled at her friends, then she swam toward the shallow water.

Morgan watched her go. She hoped that she would get to the humans before Carlos chased them too far away.

She poked her head above the water and saw Carlos had turned back toward the water. The girls were no longer shrieking or squealing. In fact, they were chasing the lobster and hissing.

Morgan smiled. Yes, they really were very brave. Maybe they didn't speak Carlos's language, but they knew how to protect themselves if they needed to—and how to work together.

Maybe the humans really would be able to help.

CHAPTER 4

As the human girls charged into the water, Bethany began to lift her head.

Morgan watched as she continued to rise until her head and shoulders were in the open air. Rachel stopped short right in front of Bethany and gasped.

Bethany gasped as well and jumped back just a little.

"It's you." Bethany stared at her with wide eyes.

"It's you." The young girl stared back at her. "I thought maybe it was all a dream. So did my friends. They will be here soon."

"It wasn't a dream." Bethany swam a little closer to her. "Please don't be afraid."

"I'm not afraid." Her voice trembled as she spoke. "I'm happy to see you again."

"I'm happy to see you again as well. But I didn't just come to visit." She took a deep breath. "I came because I need your help. We all do." She glanced over her shoulder at the other mermaids gathered close.

Each had just the top of her head and eyes above the water.

"There are more of you!" The human girl gasped. "I didn't realize." She stumbled back a few steps along the beach.

"Rachel, are you okay?" Another set of feet pounded across the sand.

Morgan turned in time to see two other human girls approach Rachel.

"They're here!" Rachel grinned at her friends as they reached her. "The mermaids! They're back!"

"Shh!" Val spoke sharply. "We don't want anyone else to hear."

"We have to make sure the mermaids stay safe." Jessie nodded.

"That's why I'm here." Bethany reached out her hand to Rachel. "Our friend Michelle has been taken. We need your help to get her back."

"Taken?" Jessie gasped. "By who?"

"She was caught in a fishing net yesterday." Bethany rubbed her fingertip along the gem on her throat.

Morgan narrowed her eyes. She sensed that Bethany didn't have much longer that she could wear the gem without losing her ability to breathe under water. As she swam close to Bethany, she wished that she could speak with the humans the way that Bethany did.

"Oh no!" Jessie clasped her hand over her mouth.

"That's terrible." Rachel shook her head. "Of course we want to help, but how can we?"

"We tried to chase after the boat, but we lost track of it." Bethany frowned. "We have no idea how to find her now. Do you know where the boat might have gone?"

"If it was a fishing boat, it would be at the dock." Jessie looked over at her friends. "It's where they all go after their fishing trips. Right, Val?"

"Right." Val stared down into the water.

"What's wrong?" Bethany swam a little closer to her. "Why do you look so sad?"

"Val's father is a fisherman," Rachel whispered.

"Don't tell her that!" Val gasped. "She'll hate me!"

"I won't hate you." Bethany shook her head. "I'm sure your father is very good at his job."

"But he catches innocent fish." She met Bethany's eyes. "Aren't you angry about that?"

"I'd have to be angry at half the creatures in the ocean if I was angry at anyone who ever ate a fish." She smiled some. "It's okay, Val. What we really need is to find our friend and get her safe before someone discovers her. Do you think that you can help us with that?"

"Yes, I do." She smiled. "I can show you where the dock is." She waded into the water. "But I'm not sure that I can swim that far."

"Don't worry, I have a friend that can help with that." Bethany smiled.

The other mermaids ducked back under the water.

"Avery, do you think Tommy will mind giving the girls a ride?" Morgan looked over at the large sea turtle.

"Not at all. But we'll have to be careful. Tommy could be in danger too if he is spotted. He's one of the largest of his kind and the humans will be quite curious about that." She patted Tommy's shell. "Do you mind helping us, Tommy?"

Tommy smiled. He swam further into the shallow water, then floated a few feet out from the shore.

"That's as close as he can get without getting stuck in the sand." Avery glanced at the others. "We'll have to help the girls out to him."

"You mean touch them?" Kira scrunched up her nose. "What if they feel funny?"

"They might be slippery." Trina cringed.

"Or slimy." Avery shuddered.

"I'm sure they think the same things about us." Morgan glanced back through the water. She could see Val's legs in the water. They did look quite strange. "But it's not their fault they don't have tails or scales. We just have to do our best to be good friends to them. Okay?"

"Okay." Trina nodded. "I can do that." She swam forward. "I'll take Val."

"And I'll take Rachel." Kira swam after her.

Bethany sank down under the water and gestured for the other mermaids to come close.

"Listen, the human girls want to help us and I think we can trust them. But Val's father is a fishermen. We need to be very careful." She looked between each of them. "And please remember, humans are fragile. They can't breathe under water. We must keep them safe."

"We will." Morgan nodded. "I'll take Jessie." She swam after Kira and Trina.

It was strange to swim toward a human, instead of away. But it was a nice kind of strange, as if she was discovering something new for the first time. She'd made so many new friends in such a short time that it was hard to believe that she'd ever been lonely.

CHAPTER 5

Getting the humans onto Tommy was not exactly as easy as the mermaids planned.

Morgan helped Jessie onto her shoulders and tried to give her a firm push up onto Tommy's slippery shell. However, each time she pushed her up onto the turtle, Jessie only slid back down and into the water. Morgan scooped her up and boosted her back up onto the shell again. This time she gave the girl a hard shove.

Jessie reached the top of the shell, then slid down the other side.

Morgan gulped and swam under the turtle to the other side of him just in time to snatch Jessie up and bring her back to the surface.

Jessie coughed and sputtered as she drew in big breaths of air.

Morgan looked through the water at the other mermaids, who were having just as much trouble, and shook her head.

"I don't think this is going to work."

"We just have to show them how to hang on." Kira swam up

to Tommy. She grabbed the edge of his shell near his head and pulled herself up on top of him.

"Kira!" Morgan cringed as she knew that Kira was fully exposed to anyone who might be walking along the beach. Seeing a mermaid or a giant sea turtle would be strange enough. But seeing a mermaid sprawled across a giant sea turtle would be a sight that no human could ignore.

"Oh, I see!" Jessie nodded as she watched Kira. She waved to Rachel and Val as Kira slid back down into the water. "We have to hold onto his shell. We can do this!" She looked down through the water at Morgan. "Let's try again."

Morgan smiled at the girl's enthusiasm. She let her climb onto her shoulders again, then swam up through the water. As Jessie climbed onto Tommy's shell, Morgan gave her a firm boost. Jessie caught the edge of Tommy's shell and held on tight with one hand. Then she reached out to Val with her other hand.

"Grab on, we can do this!"

Val smiled and grabbed her hand. Once all three humans were on Tommy's back, the turtle began to swim.

"That way." Val pointed ahead of them. She guided the turtle and the mermaids toward a long wooden structure that was dotted with several boats.

"There." Jessie crouched down against Tommy's shell and pointed at the long dock. "The boats pull in here. Usually they don't empty the nets right away. But it won't be long before they do. Do you know which boat Michelle was caught by?"

"No." Bethany sighed.

Morgan swam forward. She tugged on Bethany's hand and drew her under the water.

"I know which boat it was. At least I think I will know if I take a look at each of them. I chased it for so long that I'm sure I could pick it out if I saw it." She glanced at the others. "Just give me a few minutes to look."

"Morgan, it's too dangerous." Kira shook her head. "If you swim near the nets you could be caught in them or one of the fishermen might spot you. The water isn't very deep there."

"What choice do we have?" Morgan frowned. "Michelle is trapped in one of those nets. Who knows for how long? She's only going to get free if we are able to save her. But we can't do that if we don't figure out which boat took her."

"She's right." Bethany stared at Morgan. "I know it's dangerous, but Morgan is right. If we want to save Michelle, we're going to have to take a chance. But Morgan, you shouldn't go alone. I'll go with you."

"No, it should be me." Trina swam forward. "I'll go with Morgan."

"I'm the one with the gem, remember?" Bethany touched the gem embedded in her skin. "I might be able to use it to help us if we get into some kind of trouble."

"It still seems like a very bad idea." Kira clasped her hands together. "Maybe we should think this through a little longer."

"There isn't time." Morgan turned toward the boats. "I'm swimming over to them. Whoever wants to come with me can, but I'm not waiting any longer." She began to swim swiftly through the water.

Moments later she felt the subtle waves of a mermaid swimming beside her. She glanced over to see that it was Bethany. A moment later she felt the same thing on the other side of her and turned to see Trina as well.

Despite the dangerous situation she couldn't help but smile. She'd never really had friends before and just having two mermaids to swim at her side made her feel somehow stronger.

As she swam toward the boats, the water felt different. It felt a bit thicker and the currents both pushed and pulled at her.

She realized she'd never been in water so disrupted by the movement of boats before. As a rule, she stayed away from the dangerous machines that had sharp propellers and loud motors. It went against her instincts to swim closer to them. But she forced herself to keep going. Michelle and all of her new friends were depending on her.

"Don't get too close," Trina warned as she swam closer to Morgan. "Just try to see if you can pick out which one you followed."

Morgan narrowed her eyes. Many of the boats looked very similar. Most were white, like the one she had followed. A sick feeling bubbled up in her stomach. What if she couldn't tell? What if she couldn't pick out the right one?

She did her best to ignore her fear as she swam past each boat. One of them had to be the right one. She just had to trust that she could remember which one it was.

CHAPTER 6

After searching for a few more minutes, Morgan finally spotted what she thought was the right boat. She did her best not to doubt herself and hoped that she was right.

"It's this one." Morgan nodded as she looked at the blue stripe on the boat. "I'm sure of it. This is the one."

"Where's the net?" Bethany swam forward some. "I don't see one anywhere."

"There's a rope here." Trina grabbed it and gave a light tug. "It's attached to something heavy. The net must be further out in the water."

"We can swim out to it." Morgan began to follow the rope in the direction of the net. But as she swam alongside of it, something strange began to happen. The rope began to move. It moved toward the dock.

In the distance, she could see the net fast approaching. It was so full that it almost touched the bottom of the water.

Her stomach twisted at the thought of Michelle being stuck inside. What if she was hurt? What if she was trapped inside with dangerous creatures?

"Hurry!" Bethany called out. "They're going to raise the net out of the water. We have to get to it before they do!"

Morgan swam fast, but the rope pulled even faster.

By the time she reached the net it jerked upward through the water toward the surface.

"We're too late!" Morgan gasped as she watched the net lift up through the water. In seconds it would be out in the open air and the chance to save Michelle would be gone.

She lunged toward the net and managed to get her fingers wrapped around the rope. The net lurched for a moment, then dropped a few inches back into the water.

"Grab on!" Bethany shouted. "Maybe if we all pull, we can stop it!" She grabbed onto the net as well.

"It's worth a try!" Trina grabbed on beside Bethany.

"Tug!" Morgan cried out.

All three mermaids pulled as hard as they could.

The net sank deeper into the water. Morgan searched for any sign of Michelle, but she couldn't see her. "Where is she?"

"I don't see her." Bethany yelled. "She must have made her way to the middle for safety. We have to keep looking."

"I'm still pulling!" Trina huffed as she tightened her grasp on the net.

"It's working!" Morgan smiled with relief as the net sank down a little farther. "If we can get the ropes cut, then we can set her free." She dug her nails into the rope. "They're so strong!"

"We need a blade!" Bethany called out.

"I don't have anything like that." Trina frowned. "What about Carlos? Do you think his claws would work?"

"No, I don't think so." Morgan shook her head. "They won't be sharp enough." She looked toward the bottom of the water. "There are some broken shells in the sand. They might work. I'll be right back. Keep tugging!"

She swam down toward the shells. As she did, she caught sight of the other mermaids swimming toward them. "Grab onto the net!" she called to them. "Help hold it down!" She snatched a piece of jagged shell from the sand and swam back up toward the net. As she did, she thought it seemed further away than it had before.

"I'm tugging as hard as I can!" Avery cried out. "But the net is lifting!"

"Pull harder!" Morgan grabbed the net with one hand and used the shell to try to cut through the rope with the other. A few of the strands of rope frayed, then the shell shattered in her hand. "It's no use! It's not strong enough!" Morgan's heart pounded as the net continued to rise It neared the surface of the water.

Within seconds, not only would Michelle be hoisted in the air, but the rest of the mermaids clinging to the net would be as well.

"We have to let go!" Morgan shouted. "We won't be able to breathe once the net lifts out of the water."

"What are we going to do?" Bethany whimpered. "How are we going to get her free?"

"Let go!" Morgan cried out again as the top of the net emerged from the water.

All of the mermaids released the net, which caused it to suddenly shoot up higher into the air.

"Michelle won't be able to breathe!" Bethany fought back tears. "We have to save her! I'm going to speak to the girls!" She swam back toward Tommy.

"They're already gone." Tommy lowered his head further into the water to speak to the mermaids swimming in his direction. "They jumped off my back and swam toward the dock a few minutes ago. I watched to be sure they made it to the dock safely."

"Where are they now?" Bethany looked into his eyes.

"I'll show you." He dipped down into the water to allow her to wrap her arm around his neck.

Bethany pressed the gem against her neck, then swam to the surface with Tommy's help.

Morgan followed after them and poked her head above the water. She could see the three human girls running down the long dock toward the boat with the blue stripe. But what could they do to save Michelle? She doubted that they could prevent the fishermen from seeing the trapped mermaid.

"Girls!" Bethany called out to them. "We couldn't cut the net!"

The three human girls spun around to look at her. They waved to Bethany and Morgan, then continued to run toward the boat with the blue stripe.

Morgan didn't know what their plan was, but she knew that she needed to be nearby when they tried it.

As she swam back toward the boat, she tried to think of a way to get Michelle free. Could they tip the boat over? She doubted that even with all of their force they could do that, and if they did, there was no guarantee that Michelle wouldn't get hurt in the process.

Michelle's only chance for rescue was three human girls who had only recently discovered that mermaids actually existed. Were they really up to the challenge?

CHAPTER 7

Morgan swam right up to the side of the boat. She counted the seconds that passed by the pounding of her heartbeat. How long had Michelle been out of the water? How long could she survive without being able to breathe?

She wished that she had a gem like Bethany's that she could offer to the other mermaid. But that wasn't an option. Instead, she pushed her head up through the water right next to the boat. She watched as the three girls stopped in front of the boat.

The other mermaids gathered close around her, though only Morgan remained above the water. Bethany swam right up to the dock. She kept her head low, but she was close enough to speak to the girls if she needed to.

Val boldly took the lead as she waved to the fishermen on the boat.

"Ahoy there! What a haul!" She laughed as she looked up at the net. "I'll bet you never brought in so many fish at one time before!"

"Who is that?" A large man with a gray beard and sharp blue eyes stared at the little girl. "Oh, is that you, Val? Bill's little girl?"

"Yes, it's me." Val waved to him again. "My friends and I are having a contest. We want to see if we can guess how many fish you have in that net! But we'd really like to get a closer look before we guess. Do you think we could?" She smiled sweetly at the man.

Morgan watched as the four humans interacted. She could tell from the way they spoke to each other that they weren't enemies. But would the fisherman really grant the little girl her request?

"Alright, sure, you can have a look. But be careful. That net is about to burst. We're going to start going through it here in a few minutes. So make it snappy." He nodded his head toward the net. "Be careful on the deck, it's slippery."

"We will be." Val nodded. She glanced at her friends, then she shot a brief look toward the water.

Bethany gave her a quick wave, then ducked under the water. When she came up again, she was right beside Morgan.

"What do you think they will do?" She lowered her head under the water so that she could speak to Morgan.

"I'm not sure, but they have something in mind. I just hope it happens fast enough. Michelle might not have much time left." She frowned.

"We have to hope that she does." Bethany stuck her head above the water again, then ducked back down. "I think they're going to try to cut the net. I just saw Jessie hand Val a little blade. It looked a lot like some of the human relics we've found in the water."

"That should do it." Morgan nodded. "If I had that it would have cut right through the net."

"I just hope they can do it without getting caught." She frowned.

"I think I can help with that." Morgan smiled.

"What? How?" Bethany stared at her.

"Just stay close to the girls in case they need our help. You'll know what I'm up to when you see it." She swam away from Bethany, out further into the water. Then she zoomed right back, straight for the dock. The faster she swam, the choppier the water became.

She waited until the very last minute, then spun around so that her tail faced the dock. She splashed her tail through the water as hard and fast as she could. The movement created a flurry of waves and splashes that rolled right over the dock and struck a few fishermen as they walked across it.

"Hey!" she heard one shout.

"What's that in the water?" another hollered.

She continued to wave her tail through the water. She hoped that if all the fishermen on the dock were distracted by her water show, then the girls would have time to cut through the net.

But what then? Would they be able to get Michelle into the water? Would Michelle be able to get herself into the water? Morgan had no idea what to expect.

Exhausted from all of the splashing, she swam deeper into the water, then right back up through it. As she flipped her tail again, she didn't pay as close attention to hiding it.

"It's a fish! Some kind of massive fish!" one of the fishermen on the dock shouted.

"Get the nets!" another one called out.

Morgan's heart skipped a beat. Had she just put all the mermaids in danger by drawing attention to the water? If the fishermen began to throw their nets, they were sure to snag a few mermaids, a giant sea turtle, and maybe even a lobster.

"Jasper, warn the others!" Morgan shooed him off toward the other mermaids. She stopped splashing her tail. Maybe the fishermen would lose interest. As she swam close to the boat with the blue stripe, she poked her head just enough above the water to spot the three human girls.

Jessie was hard at work with the blade, trying to cut the rope.

"Get the girls on the dock!" a woman shouted from somewhere on the dock. "With that monster in the water, it's not safe on the boats!"

Morgan's heart sank as she realized the girls were about to be caught. What would the fishermen do to them if they found them sabotaging their net? She wasn't sure what to expect from the humans, but she knew she didn't want the human helpers hurt.

Bethany ducked down under the water.

"What are we going to do, Morgan?"

Morgan had to think fast. She knew that she had to do something to distract the humans enough that they would forget for even a few seconds about the human girls on the boat. She could only think of one thing that would shock them that much.

"Bethany, you and the others get as far from the dock as possible." Morgan met her eyes.

"But what if the girls need me?" Bethany stared back at her.

"Just trust me and do what I ask!" Morgan swam off, back toward the dock.

CHAPTER 8

Morgan could only hope that Bethany would listen to her. There wasn't time to think up another plan or make another choice. There was only one thing that she could try.

As she neared the dock, she swam deep under the water to the sand below. Then she used her tail to launch herself up off of the sand and straight into the air. As her head broke through the surface of the water, a shiver went through her whole body. She was about to be seen by several humans all at once and she had no idea what the sighting might lead to.

As her body continued to travel past the surface of the water and through the air, she flicked her tail hard to give herself one last push up into the air. For a few seconds, she sailed above the water, her body curved and her tail in full view.

She heard gasps, shrieks, and shouts. She heard the sound of people scrambling to get closer.

Her stomach flipped, both with fear and with the fun of the sensation of flying. She had never experienced it before and as she crashed back down into the water, she already missed it.

She'd never felt anything so thrilling. She knew in that moment that she'd done two things. She'd proven to everyone who looked her way that mermaids existed and she'd distracted the humans. But was it long enough for the girls to cut through the net?

She looked through the water and caught sight of Bethany, still close to the boat with the blue stripe.

"I told you to get away from here!" Morgan frowned as she swam swiftly over to her.

"I couldn't leave you—or Jessie, Val, and Rachel." Bethany stared at her with wide eyes. "I can't believe you just did that. You are so brave!"

"Foolish, don't you mean?" Morgan shook her head. "I just hope it bought them enough time to cut the net."

"I'll take a look." Bethany began to break the surface.

"Careful." Morgan caught her hand and swam up with her. "They'll be looking at the water now.

Luckily the shadow cast by the edge of the boat gave them a safe place to peek above the water.

Morgan heard a loud splatter and thump and looked in the direction of the net just in time to see the last of its contents sprawl across the deck of the ship.

"Do you see it?" Several fishermen had gathered on the dock. "Is it still out there? It was real, wasn't it?"

The men and women shouted at each other, confused and excited by the sight of a real mermaid.

"It must have been some kind of trick!" One of the women shook her head. "Everyone knows that mermaids are not real!"

Morgan couldn't help but smile to herself, but her attention returned to Michelle. Though she searched through the pile of fish and other creatures, she didn't see any sign of the mermaid. However, she did hear a loud shout.

"What did you do!" The fisherman who'd allowed the girls onto the boat stormed across the deck in their direction. "How did this happen?" His voice grew even louder.

"It was an accident!" Val cried out as she stepped in front of Jessie. "We were just looking and it burst open!"

"Burst open you say?" He grabbed the net that still hung in the air and peered at the rope that had been cut. "Rope doesn't tear like this. You must have cut it! Empty your pockets now!" He stared at the three of them.

"We didn't!" Rachel called out. Her hands shook as she reached into her pockets.

"Oh no," Morgan whispered under the water. She could see the blade still clutched in Jessie's hand. If she dropped it, it would surely make a sound against the smooth hard surface of the deck. It would only be a matter of seconds before the fisherman discovered it.

"You!" The fisherman pointed at Jessie. "What do you have in your hand?"

"Leave her alone!" Val put her hands on her hips. "Or I'll tell my father how you treated us!"

"Oh, don't you worry, little lady." The fisherman put his hands on his hips as he glared at her. "I'll be speaking to your father about this myself!"

"This is terrible." Morgan sank further under the water. "Now the girls are in trouble—big trouble—and Michelle wasn't even in there!"

"She must have been. You said it was this boat, right?" Bethany met her eyes.

"I thought it was." Morgan's chin began to tremble. "But maybe—maybe I was wrong." A horrible feeling filled her stomach at the thought of Michelle trapped in another net attached to another boat.

"We've got to do something to help them." Bethany pushed up through the water again. She began to bang on the side of the boat.

Morgan swam up beside her and did the same.

"Now what is that?" The fisherman barked. "You!" He pointed his finger at Jessie. "Open up your hand and show me what you're hiding!"

Morgan banged on the side of the boat as hard as she could.

"I don't have anything," Jessie whimpered and took a step back from the fisherman.

"Now what is that racket?" The fisherman stomped over to the edge of the boat.

Morgan grabbed Bethany by the arm and pulled her under the water just as the fisherman looked down at them. He growled, then turned back to the girls.

Morgan poked her head above the water just in time to see the fisherman grab Jessie by the wrist. He gave her hand a hard shake and the blade dropped out of her hand.

"I knew it!" he shouted. "I knew that the three of you were up to something! Now you're all going to pay!"

"Stop!" a voice shouted. "Take your hands off her right this instant!"

Bethany gasped as she met Morgan's eyes. "That's Michelle!"

CHAPTER 9

Morgan lifted her head a little further above the water as she tried to catch sight of Michelle. She sat up in the middle of the fish and sea creatures piled around her and smacked her tail sharply against the deck of the boat.

"I said let go of her!"

The fisherman stumbled back. He sucked down huge gulps of air. Then he slipped and landed flat on his bottom a few feet away from Michelle.

The commotion had drawn the attention of other people on the dock. Many began to gather nearby for a closer look.

Morgan stared at Michelle. How could she breathe? How could she speak? Then she noticed the gem on her neck. Her eyes widened as she realized that when Michelle came looking for the others, she must have taken her gem with her. That was how she had survived her time in the net when it was outside of the water. But now she was fully exposed. Morgan had shown off by jumping in and out of the water, but Michelle was right in arm's reach of a dangerous man and several other curious people.

"We have to get her off that boat." Morgan looked over at Bethany. "They'll capture her if we don't help her."

"But how?" Bethany stared up through the water. "The boat is too large for us to tip it. The deck will be too slippery for Michelle to get herself over the railing."

"We'll have to work together. With everyone." Morgan frowned. "You stay here and watch Michelle. I will swim quickly to get the others."

"I'll keep an eye on her but be as fast as you can." Bethany frowned.

"I will be!" Morgan began to swim through the water, faster than she even knew she could. The further she swam, the harder her heart pounded. Had they already caged Michelle? How long had she had the gem in her neck? What if she'd already reached the point where she couldn't breathe under water?

Morgan reached the other mermaids not far from the dock.

"We have to work together to save Michelle." She filled them in on what had happened as they swam back toward the boat.

Tommy eyed it. "I could push it."

"Pushing it won't be enough." Morgan shook her head.

"Maybe if we all swam under it?" Kira raised an eyebrow. "Maybe we could rock it enough to at least knock the human off it?"

"Knocking one human off won't help much. There are too many of them." Morgan paused as she reached Bethany's side. She gave the other mermaid's tail a light tap. "What's going on up there? Is she okay?"

Bethany sank down to speak to her. "Michelle is still there. The girls have surrounded her and aren't letting the fisherman get near her. But the crowd is getting restless. Someone said they were going to find Val's father."

"Oh no." Morgan frowned. "Now she'll be in even more trouble. There's only one thing I can think to do, but we'll have to get Jessie's blade."

"What is your plan?" Trina swam close to her.

"If we can get the blade, we can cut the boat free from its anchor and the dock. Then between all of us and Tommy we can push the boat out into the water. Then at least we would only have one human to deal with." She frowned. "But it's risky. If we don't do everything just right, we could all get caught."

"I can get the blade." Bea, the sea slug perched on Trina's shoulder, crawled forward. "I can go right up the side of the boat and across the deck. No one will even notice me."

"That's a great idea." Morgan nodded. "Bring it right back to me."

"Be careful, Bea." Trina swam up to the side of the boat so that Bea could climb onto it.

The sea slug slimed her way up the side of the boat and over the edge of it. She squeezed under the railing and headed straight for the blade that had been knocked out of Jessie's hand.

The fisherman had gotten back to his feet and his focus was now on Michelle in the middle of all his fish.

"You can't be real." He stared at her. "This can't be happening. Am I dreaming?" He glanced at the three human girls. "Is this some kind of prank you're playing? Val, when your father gets here, he's going to have plenty to say about this!"

"It isn't a prank." Val stepped forward. "Please, she needs our help. She can't be out of the water for long."

"Oh, we'll get her a tank for sure. Bud!" he shouted back to the dock. "Bud, bring me that lobster tank you've got! I think she'll fit in there! Hurry!"

Morgan shuddered at the thought of Michelle being wedged into a tank. She watched as Bea crept closer to the edge of the boat with the blade in tow.

"Please hurry," she whispered. Then she looked at the others. "We all have to be ready to push once I cut the ropes."

"What's going on here?" another angry voice blasted through the water.

Morgan returned to the surface and watched as a man strode past the crowd and onto the boat. She winced. Another human complicated things.

Bea nudged the blade over the edge of the boat.

Morgan grabbed it before it could sink too far in the water. She hurried to the rope attached to the anchor and quickly sliced through it. Then she swam to the rope that tied the boat to the dock. This one was harder to cut, as it was mostly out of the water. She worked as fast as she could.

"Your daughter and her friends are up to something here for sure." The fisherman spoke to the other man. "They won't tell me what, but it looks to me that we've caught ourselves a real live mermaid. Bud is bringing me a tank for her."

"A tank?" The taller man stared at Michelle. "Val, are you okay? Girls?" He looked at the young girls that surrounded the mermaid.

"Daddy, please." Val stared into his eyes. "We promised to help protect them. She needs our help. She has to get back in the water!"

"Now!" Michelle shouted to the other mermaids and Tommy. "Start pulling now!"

The boat lurched so hard that all the humans on the deck slipped and fell.

CHAPTER 10

"Faster!" Morgan cried out as she pushed on the boat as hard as she could.

Once it began to move, it became easier to push. Tommy's strength and size was a big help. From the shouts and shrieks that echoed through the water, she guessed that the people on the dock had spotted him as well. But there was no time to worry about that. All she could think about was getting Michelle to safety. Unfortunately, with two adult humans on the boat, that would be a bit harder.

Once they were out into deeper water and far enough away from the other humans, Morgan dared to break the surface and look onto the boat.

Val, Jessie, and Rachel held onto the railing near Michelle. Val's father and the fisherman had managed to regain their balance.

"This is so amazing." Val's father stared at Michelle. "She looks just like a little girl." He glanced at Val. "She looks like she could be your age."

"That's because she is, Daddy!" Val let go of the railing and walked over to him. "She's a young mermaid and she needs her family. Please, we have to help her."

"No way." The fisherman laughed. "This little sea-beast is going to make me a rich man! I'll get us back to the dock." He started toward the front of the boat.

"Are you okay?" Val's father looked at Michelle. "Are you hurt?"

"I'm not hurt." Michelle stared back at him. "Not yet."

Bethany broke the surface and clung onto the side of the ship.

"Michelle!" she called out. "Michelle, we have to get you back in the water!"

"Wow!" Val's father jumped back. "There's more of you?"

"Many more." Bethany looked over the side of the boat at him. "We may look like creatures to you, but we are more than that. Please, let us help our friend."

"Daddy, you can't let her end up in a tank! Please!" Val grabbed his hand.

Val's father looked toward the fisherman, who'd started the engine of the boat, then he looked back at his daughter.

"Hurry," he whispered. "We'll have to move very quickly." He crouched down and reached his arms out to Michelle.

Michelle shied back and slid across the deck of the boat.

Morgan could understand why she was afraid.

"It's okay." Val crouched down beside her and took her hand. Rachel and Jessie crouched down close to her as well. "He's going to help you, I promise."

Morgan wondered if that would be true. Wasn't he a fisherman? Wasn't he a human that might think they were monsters?

"Trust him, Michelle," Bethany called out to her. "Let him help you!"

Michelle bit into her bottom lip but nodded.

Morgan shivered as she watched the human pick Michelle up.

"Hey! What are you doing with her?" the fisherman shouted from forward on the boat.

"Hurry, Dad!" Val shouted as she and her friends formed a wall between the fisherman and Val's father.

The man who carried Michelle lifted her over the railing and eased her down into the water beside Bethany.

"Don't you do that! Don't you dare!" the fisherman shouted.

All of the mermaids and even Tommy lifted their heads above the water to watch as Bethany wrapped Michelle up in her arms.

"Thank you!" Bethany called out to Val's father. "Thank you all!"

"We need to go!" Morgan tugged on Bethany's tail until she was under the water. "The boat is dangerous and so are all the other ones headed straight for us!"

The other humans on the dock had decided to get a closer look at the mermaids.

Morgan and Tommy led the way out of the harbor as fast as they could.

"Michelle, are you okay?" Bethany held her hand tightly in hers. "Can you breathe?"

Michelle nodded and rubbed her neck. "It hurts a little, but yes I can breathe. I came looking for you, and when I got caught in that net, I thought I was done for! Thank you so much for saving me."

"We couldn't have done it without the help of the humans." Morgan looked back over her shoulder. "Now they know we're real."

"I'm going to have a lot to explain to my mother." Michelle shook her head.

When they made it back to Eldoris, Queen Maris summoned them all into the Coral Palace.

As Michelle explained everything that had happened, Morgan prepared herself. Surely the queen would be quite angry with her. She would likely tell her to leave Eldoris and never return.

"And you?" The queen looked straight at her. "You are Morgan, from the great beyond?"

"Yes." Morgan tried to sound brave.

"Morgan, we would like to welcome you to Eldoris." Queen Maris smiled at her as she swam toward her. "You may come and go from our safe haven as you please, and I do hope that you'll be willing to share with us some of your experiences and knowledge from living in the beyond."

"I would be happy to do that." Morgan smiled at her in return. "I appreciate your offer, Queen Maris."

"It is the least I can do after the part you played in bringing my daughter home safely." She looked over at Michelle, then turned back to Morgan. "In the future, however, if you have an idea that you think might improve things for all mermaid-kind, maybe you could run it by me first. I promise to keep an open heart and an open mind on the matter and perhaps we will be able to work things out together."

"I would like that." Morgan nodded.

"Now that the humans know about us, we're going to need to work extra hard, both to stay safe and to help the humans protect the world we share. I'm so glad that you will be able to help us with that, Morgan." The queen snapped her fingers, then opened her hand. "I have one more gem that I think you could put to very good use."

The queen held the gem out to Morgan. "These gems were collected from the deepest parts of the ocean in all directions. Our mermaid ancestors were great explorers and they made it their mission to discover every part of the sea that they could. These gems were studied by great mermaid minds until their secrets were unlocked and passed down from generation to generation. I know that their purpose is to unite mermaids and humans once and for all. Perhaps there was a time when we once all lived together. Eldoris was meant to protect us all. It was never meant to separate us. Now might be the time to get back to that kind of unity." She looked into Morgan's eyes. "I would like you to take this and use it to strengthen our connection with the humans."

"Thank you so much." Morgan stared at the gem as she took it from the queen's palm. "I promise I will use it to help mermaids and humans in any way that I can."

Not only had they united the mermaids and the humans, Morgan finally felt as if she was a part of Eldoris and that the mermaids of Eldoris could be a part of the great beyond as well.

ALSO BY PJ RYAN

Amazon.com/author/pjryan

*Visit the author page to save big on special bundled sets!

Additional Series:

The Fairies of Sunflower Grove

The Mermaids of Eldoris

Rebekah - Girl Detective

RJ - Boy Detective

Mouse's Secret Club

Rebekah, Mouse & RJ Special Editions

Jack's Big Secret

AVAILABLE IN AUDIO

PJ Ryan books for kids are also available as audiobooks.

Visit the author website for a complete list at: PJRyanBooks.com

You can also listen to free audio samples there.

Made in the USA
Las Vegas, NV
28 September 2021

31299209R00149